# TWO VANDALS AND A WEDDING

# Two Vandals and a Wedding

FRED SECOMBE

HarperCollins*Publishers*

HarperCollins*Publishers*
77–85 Fulham Palace Road, London W6 8JB
www.fireandwater.com

First published in Great Britain in 2000
by HarperCollins*Publishers*
1 3 5 7 9 10 8 6 4 2

A catalogue record for this book is
available from the British Library.

ISBN 0 00 628162 1

Printed and bound in Great Britain by
Creative Print and Design (Wales), Ebbw Vale

# Two Vandals and a Wedding

'Here we go again!' exclaimed William Evans, Vicar of Llanybedw. 'God versus Mammon in the annual contest with no holds barred.' He was standing at the door of my church hall and shook hands with me warmly. It was my first Ruridecanal Conference as Rural Dean. For weeks I had been dreading the occasion. Clergy and laity met to discuss matters relevant to the deanery including, most importantly, the allocation to the various parishes of the financial quota imposed on the deanery by the Board of Finance. Will had been my friend ever since I came to Abergelly and had canvassed assiduously to secure my election to my present position.

'Don't look so worried, Fred,' he said. 'I should sit back if I were you and let them tear themselves to pieces. I expect your little committee have done their best to make a fair job of their assessment. In the end, even the most militant lot will have to come to heel, with a few adjustments here and there maybe.'

The principal factor in deciding the share of the financial burden was the number of Easter communicants in each parish, with other considerations thrown in, such as the financial commitments and the social background involved. The more affluent parishes would find it easy to discharge their obligations, while those in a deprived neighbourhood would face a daunting struggle to pay their quota. There was one other unspoken qualification involved in the equation, and that was the work rate of the parish priest. Occasionally there would be one or two with a cure of souls who were oblivious of those who lived outside the Vicarage, and whose only contact with them was when couples knocked on the door to put their banns in or when the undertaker called to arrange a funeral.

As I stood at the table, which was covered with a brand new baize cloth provided by the Mothers' Union, I watched the invasion of the militants, who came with the light of battle in their eyes. They seemed to outnumber the rest of the deanery, who sauntered into the hall laughing and joking. Tobias Thomas, the portly deanery clerk, went among the throng handing out the agenda for the meeting and nomination papers for the election of lay members to the Diocesan Conference. What had incensed the malcontents this year was the steep rise in quota. This was necessary, we were told by the Board of Finance, because of the priority given to the increase of clergy stipends. Since the average amount paid to incumbents at this time was in the region of £500 per annum, it would appear that the increment would not provide the reverend gentlemen with an excess of luxury. Moreover, some of those who would rise to their feet to object to the increase in quota would be well-paid workers whose take-home pay would be considerably greater than what would come into the pockets of their parish priests.

When the church hall clock, recently repaired, indicated that it was half past seven, I rose to my feet after banging on the table with my copy of the Constitution of the Church of Wales and called the assembly to prayer. It took a few minutes to end the scraping of chairs on the floor and the clearing of tonsils. I waited until there was complete silence. After the recitation of responses and the Lord's Prayer, I repeated one of my favourite collects with all the sincerity that I could muster (and with my eyes closed tight): 'O God, forasmuch as without Thee, we are not able to please Thee, mercifully grant that Thy Holy Spirit may in all things direct and rule our hearts, through Jesus Christ our Lord, Amen.'

It was a motley mixture of lay and clerical members of the conference facing me when I opened my eyes. For example, there was the unsmiling visage of the Reverend K.J. Whittle, staring through his large horn-rimmed glasses into infinity. He was a north-countryman stranded in Wales and apparently resentful of the fact. Vicar of one of the more affluent parishes in the deanery, instantly recognizable in any gathering of the clergy by his pin-striped trousers and his grey spats, he looked like a solicitor's clerk who had come to the wrong meeting. Tom Beynon, my people's warden, had nicknamed him 'On a point of order', his constant refrain at every conference, be it ruridecanal or diocesan. Sitting in the row of chairs behind him was Harry Thompson, shop steward at Abergelly Steelworks. A burly bully of a man, red-faced and bald-headed, he was the bane of his vicar's life in the parish of Penysacoed. These two men's voices would be heard without fail whenever they were present. It was a most unpleasing prospect.

I was about to call on Tobias Thomas to read the minutes of the last meeting when I remembered that I had forgotten to pray for the soul of my predecessor, since this was the first meeting since his decease. 'Before we have the minutes of the last meeting,' I announced, 'shall we all stand in silence to honour the memory of the late Rural Dean who gave such yeoman service to the deanery over the past seven years?' My tongue was firmly in my cheek.

Once again there was a cacophony of chair movement among those who were reluctant to rise for the second time in the space of a minute. By the time I had prayed for the faithful departed, the assembly was more than ready to be seated for the rest of the evening. The secretary read the minutes at such a speed that it left him out of breath and purple-faced at its close. 'Would someone like to propose that the minutes should be approved?' I asked.

The Reverend K.J. Whittle rose to his feet. 'On a point of order, Mr Rural Dean,' he remarked, in an accent more appropriate to Huddersfield than Abergelly, 'I fail to see how we can approve something which was read so quickly that it was unintelligible.'

The secretary's face was now a deep purple. It was his turn to rise to his feet. 'Mr Rural Dean,' he spluttered, 'I have been reading these minutes for the past six years and no one has complained until now. There is no difference in the way I read them today than I have previously.'

As I tried frantically to think of a way to end this impasse, I was saved from any further embarrassment by the intervention of my good friend Will Evans. 'Mr Rural Dean,' he proclaimed in his deep Paul Robeson voice, 'I was able to follow what was read out by the secretary.' Several others nodded their agreement. 'Perhaps if the Vicar of Pontyglais had been born this side of Offa's Dyke he would have had no trouble in understanding what was said.' There was some muted laughter at this sally. The Reverend K.J. Whittle was not very popular in the deanery. I decided to ask for a show of hands on the intelligibility of the reading by Tobias Thomas. There was an almost unanimous vote that Tobias was understood. The only adverse reaction came from the Vicar and churchwardens of Pontyglais.

'I propose that we approve of the minutes as a true record,' said Will Evans. He was seconded by Ivor Hodges, my churchwarden. The motion was carried with only three abstentions.

Minor items on the agenda aroused no discussion. Everyone was waiting for the all-important matter of the allocation of the quota to arrive. 'Item number seven,' I said nervously. There was an expectant hush. 'The Committee has worked long and hard to produce a fair sharing of the burden of the quota which we have to raise as a deanery,' I went on. 'I think they are to be congratulated on the way in which they have decided on the following list, which I shall read to you.' My hand shook as I picked up the piece of paper. The complete silence was unnerving.

There was little audible reaction to the first four or five allocations, but when I came to the parish of Penysacoed, I coughed as I was about to launch into the deep. I could feel Harry Thompson's eyes boring into my face. '£320,' I managed to say in strangulated tones.

'Daylight robbery!' exploded the malcontent. For a man of his size his high-pitched voice came as a shock when first heard. To his listeners at the meeting it was depressingly familiar. I ignored the interruption and carried on with the remainder of the list. There were a few murmurs during the reading, but nothing more.

'Now then,' I said as I sat down, 'the meeting is open for discussion.' It was the starting signal for a rush of competitors to be the first to speak, but I gave them no chance. 'Since Mr Thompson has made his feelings known by his interruption, perhaps he would like to expand on his "daylight robbery" assertion.' Rather than have a large volcano simmering while others spoke, I felt it would be wiser to let it erupt at the beginning; after that it might be possible to have a reasonable debate. Having crossed the Rubicon of the list, I was feeling more confident.

'I don't know what your committee was thinking about when they drew up that list,' he began, 'but I tell you what, they don't know Penysacoed. Our congregation are mostly old age pensioners – not only that, but we've got a debt of £700 to pay off for the repair of the roof we 'ad done at the beginning of this year.' He looked around the meeting. ''Ow would some of you like to 'ave water pouring down on your 'eads in the middle of the service? One bride was drenched last December when she was standing up by the altar. That's what it's been like. It's not fair to our vicar, 'oo's doing 'is best.'

Little Isaiah Jenkins, his vicar, was sitting with his head buried in his hands, most likely praying that his church-warden would shut up. It was a vain prayer if that is what it was: Harry Thompson was in full flow. We were given a heart-rending account of how the elderly members of the congregation were going without some of the essentials of life to keep the church going. As the amount of coughing

6

and sighing increased during his peroration, he became aware that his audience were bored by the sound of his voice and his constant repetitions. 'Well, to put it in a nutshell …' he said.

'Some nutshell!' commented Will Evans loudly, provoking a burst of laughter.

'You can laugh,' went on the shop steward, 'but you will be laughing the other side of your face when we don't pay the quota.' With that threat he brought his diatribe to an end and sat down so violently that his chair must have suffered terminal damage.

He was followed by a succession of clergy and laity indulging in special pleading. Finally Ivor Hodges rose to his feet. 'Mr Rural Dean, I have never witnessed such an exhibition of self-pity in all my life as we have had during this last half hour or so. This is not the Church Militant but the Church Pathetic. Here in Abergelly we face the huge task of raising the many thousands of pounds to build a church on a neglected housing estate. That does not stop us from paying our share of the quota. That should be the priority for every parish. I propose that we accept the committee's recommended figures.' This time it was Will Evans' turn to second the motion.

There had been an embarrassed silence throughout Ivor's little speech. It continued as I asked them to vote on the proposition. One by one hands went up in support of the motion. The only votes against came from the parish of Penysacoed.

When the meeting was over, Will Evans came up to me and patted me on the back. 'Well, Mr Rural Dean, you should feel quite pleased with yourself, first for coming through your baptism of fire unscathed and second for choosing such a persuasive warden as Ivor Hodges. As your Uncle Will told you before the meeting, they would have to come to heel eventually. Mind, I didn't expect that to happen as quickly as it did, thanks to Ivor.'

'He's not a head teacher for nothing, Will,' I replied. 'He addressed the meeting as if it were an unruly school assembly.'

'Perhaps you could lend him to me for my next Parochial Church Council meeting,' my friend remarked.

'I think the Vicar of Penysacoed is more in need of him than you,' I said. 'He is the only one who would be able to put down the high and mighty Harry Thompson from his seat, apart from you. I am sure you rule your PCC with a rod of iron, tempered, of course, with an abundance of wit.'

'Flattery will get you nowhere, Mr Rural Dean!' he retorted.

'Well?' asked my wife when I returned to the Vicarage, 'How did the meeting go? Not that I need ask, I can see the light of victory in your eyes – a far different face from the one which left the house a couple of hours ago in fear and trembling. Sit down, my dear, and I shall pour you a libation worthy of a conquering hero.'

Eleanor was a family doctor. Her practice was on the Brynfelin housing estate, where we were pledged to build a permanent church to replace the temporary building. She led a busy life, not only as an overworked physician but also as the mother of two children, David, aged eight and Elspeth aged five. Her hectic life was somewhat mitigated by the invaluable assistance of our housekeeper, Mrs Cooper, whose competence was enlivened by her endless malapropisms. As I told her of the saga of self-pity initiated by Harry Thompson's diatribe and developed by a succession of other parochial representatives, she asked, 'How did you cope with that successfully, *mon petit*? Was it a blinding flash of inspiration or some other form of divine intervention?'

'Unless you would give Ivor Hodges divine status,' I replied, 'it was neither. He waited until the queue of complainants had finished their boring litany. By the time he had finished his contribution to the debate, there was complete silence. He began by saying that he had never witnessed such an exhibition of self-pity in all his life and finished by proposing that the meeting should accept the proposed sharing of the quota. The only votes against came from the Harry Thompson contingent. It was fantastic.'

'You can say that again,' she commented. She handed me a large whisky. I was about to imbibe when she ordered me to hold on to my glass until she had poured a helping for herself, which was equally generous. 'Here's to good old Ivor,' she proclaimed. 'Without him we would have been drowning our sorrows instead of celebrating a victory.'

The next morning after Matins at the parish church, Hugh Thomas, my curate, was full of praise for Ivor Hodges. Hugh had come to me as an ordinand, full of self-confidence, ready to turn the world upside down in the first year of his ministry. An athletic young man with a promising future as an outside half playing for Abergelly, who were in the top rank of Welsh rugby, he had sacrificed his chances of glory to settle down to a future of domestic bliss with his fiancée, the organist at the daughter church where he was in charge. Janet Rees was a clerk in the local council offices. Like my wife, who had been given a council house to act as a surgery on the Brynfelin estate, Janet and her intended were promised a place after their proposed marriage. Hugh was a diligent parish priest and an effective preacher who, like his vicar, delivered his sermons without a script, occasionally finding, also like his superior, that he was enclosed in a field without a gate for escape.

'What a little gem of a speech that was!' he remarked. 'In the space of a few minutes he disposed of an hour's waffle from the previous speakers and won the day for you.'

'I think there is a moral for us both, Hugh, in that little gem,' I replied. 'Short and sweet in the pulpit is much more effective than ponderous oratory.'

'Point taken, Vicar,' he said.

Our conversation in the vestry was interrupted by a loud knock on the vestry door. 'Come in!' I shouted. To my consternation there appeared the imposing figure of John Trengrove, police constable and second-row forward in the Abergelly first fifteen and erstwhile colleague of my curate.

'Hallo, Hugh!' he said, and then turned his attention to me. 'Vicar, I'm afraid I have to report a break-in at Hugh's church. The altar has been desecrated, with the wooden cross chopped up and the purple hanging cloth partly burnt. They've poured communion wine everywhere. The chairs have been badly damaged, and the prayer books and hymn books all torn apart. It's a real mess, I can tell you. We thought, first of all, that it must have been kids, but the Superintendent thinks it is something more serious than that. It must be somebody with a grudge against religion. I think you must come and have a look for yourself.

I've got a police car outside. The Super is up in the church, so if you'd both like to come with me you can see for yourselves what has happened.'

Ten minutes later my curate and I were surveying the devastation, in company with the police superintendent, Brian Williams. It was a shock to see the little tabernacle, so revered by the faithful few who worshipped there, savaged in such a fashion.

'Kids wouldn't chop up the cross,' said the Superintendent. 'That's the work of some kind of crank, and a very dangerous kind of crank. The sooner we get him the better, otherwise it will be your church next, Vicar, believe me. Yes, I'm afraid you will have to organize an all-night watch, not to mention an all-day one. Perhaps you can warn all your churches in the Abergelly area to do the same. In the meanwhile, we shall make enquiries as best we can to trace any suspect, but I'm afraid I don't have much hope of success at the moment. If you hear of anyone acting suspiciously in the vicinity of your church, let us know immediately.

'I'm sorry to say that the next episode in this catalogue of incidents could be a church being burnt down. You can see that he did attempt to start a fire. If he attacks another church, it won't be wine that he sprinkles around, but petrol. In that case it would be disastrous.'

'Bloody hell!' A shout from the back of the church ended the Superintendent's remarks. It came from the churchwarden at St David's, Dai Elbow, former notorious back-row forward in the local rugby team and shift worker at the colliery. David Rees had been banned permanently from the game because of the dangerous use of his elbow, which had laid low several opponents. He was now a devoted churchman and a pillar of the congregation.

Dai strode down the aisle and confronted the Superintendent. 'I 'ope you're going to catch the bugger that's done this as soon as possible, Mr Williams. It's only fair to the rate-payers that the sooner 'e's been put be'ind bars, the better.'

'Now then, Dai,' said the officer, 'calm down. If you'd kept your temper you could have been playing for Abergelly a lot longer.'

I thought Dai was about to explode and use his elbow on the embodiment of the law. He looked at me and I shook my head.

'What we have to do is to make sure that this is not going to happen again,' went on Brian Williams. 'I have been telling the Vicar that he must organize teams of men to keep watch night and day until we find who is responsible. I am afraid that is the only way to protect the buildings from this madman. Your church and all the other churches around here are going to depend upon you and your congregation to prevent any further destruction. The police force has only a limited number of men, and they have many other duties to perform. We shall do our best, and it is up to you to do your best.' With that warning he turned on his heel and made his way out of the church.

As he went, Dai Elbow took off his jacket and began to collect the hymn books and prayer books. 'Come on, Hugh,' he commanded, 'let's get stuck into this.'

'Hold on, Dai,' said PC Trengrove. 'I've got to take the Curate and the Vicar down to Abergelly.'

'That's right,' I added. 'My wife will be wondering what has happened, and I expect Hugh hasn't had his breakfast yet. I suggest you organize a working party later today. What's more, you will have to get a rota of fire-watchers as the Superintendent suggests.'

'Fat lot of good that will be!' he retorted. 'That's like locking up the stable once the 'orse 'as bolted.'

'I'll meet you here at ten o'clock,' said my curate. 'In the meanwhile, if you can collect some volunteers who are on the afternoon shift, so much the better.' We left him gathering the books, muttering to himself what must have been unprintable epithets, quite inappropriate in a church.

When I arrived at the Vicarage my wife's car had gone. Mrs Cooper opened the front door for me before I could use my key. 'Dr Secombe says to tell you that she couldn't wait any longer and would you contact her at the surgery to let her know what has happened.'

'I should think that by the time she gets to Brynfelin all her patients will be passing on the bad news,' I replied. 'Somebody has broken into the church and done a lot of damage.'

Our housekeeper's eyes opened wide. 'Well!' she exclaimed. 'Children! Who'd have 'em?'

'I'm afraid it's not children, Mrs Cooper. It's much more serious than that. It's a grown-up, the police think.'

Her eyes opened even wider. 'That's frightening, that is. He must be one of those wot-you-calls.' She went into the kitchen shaking her head.

Sure enough, when I rang Eleanor she had been fully informed by her patients about the damage inflicted on St David's. 'The police Superintendent wants all the churches in the deanery to keep a day and night watch. I have to ask them to make a rota of volunteers. He is convinced that this maniac will strike again and this time would burn a church to the ground,' I told her.

'Rubbish!' she said sharply. 'Whoever did it must have known that there was a wooden cross on the altar and to that end brought a hatchet to chop it up. St David's must be the only church not to have a brass cross. I think he's making a big fuss over an idiot who has some kind of grudge about that particular building. You've got enough work on your plate without having to ring around all the churches in the neighbourhood. In any case, most of them will ignore his advice, I expect.'

'Listen, Sherlock Holmes,' I retorted, 'if the police have told me to take these precautions I can't ignore the advice. I shall ring the parishes now and then go to see Tom Beynon afterwards to ask him to organize a rota for the parish church.'

'I think you're mad!' she said and put the phone down. The response I had from the incumbents was very mixed. Some of them shared Eleanor's opinion and said that while they would keep an eye open for anyone acting suspiciously, they could not go to the length of organizing rotas. Uncle Will was one of those.

'I know Brian Williams quite well. He was a parishioner of mine once, before he rose to the eminence of Superintendent. He likes to exert his authority. Anyway, Frederick, you have far too much to do without having to waste your time ringing twenty incumbents. You will be lucky if you get half a dozen who will obey his call.'

He was right: only six of them said that they would 'do

something about it'. By the time I had completed my marathon task, it was past twelve o'clock. I decided to go to see the people's warden before he went to work on the two till ten shift.

Tom Beynon had been a miner since he left school. His face wore the blue scars which were the trademarks of the mining profession. He was the kind of man who looked you in the eyes when he spoke to you and whose word you could always trust. Tom had been the people's warden for fifteen years, but had never assumed that the position was one which was his by right. When I had arrived, four years earlier, I had suggested that it might be good for the parish if there was a change of wardens every five years. 'I am sure you are right, Vicar,' he had said when I broached the subject in my enthusiasm to make all things new. Now after four years of working with someone who knew the parish of Abergelly so intimately and who was held in such high regard, not only by the congregation but by the people who never appeared in church, I felt diminished that I had made such a brash proposition. My only hope was that Tom had forgotten that ill-advised remark. However, knowing him, I was sure that as the five-year limit grew ever closer, he would remind me of the doomsday I had imposed upon him. Very soon it would be the Easter Vestry and the congregation would be asked to elect their representative. With just one more year to reach the deadline, I would be faced with the loss of someone who was indispensable in the office of people's warden.

'Vicar! How nice to see you.' He greeted me like a long-lost friend despite the fact that he had been with me at the

Ruridecanal Conference the night before. I was ushered into the front room and regaled with a glass of stout.

'That was a great piece of work by Ivor last night,' he commented, as we sat down in the two large armchairs which faced the bow window. 'I don't suppose this is a social call,' he went on, 'so spill out the beans, as they do say in America. I can see by the look on your face that something serious has happened.'

'I'm afraid it has,' I replied. 'Some maniac has broken into St David's and has caused a large amount of damage. He has chopped up the altar cross, tried to burn the frontal, torn up hymn books and prayer books, broken several chairs and poured communion wine all over the place. The police superintendent thinks that he is likely to strike again and could possibly burn a church down. He has asked me to tell all the incumbents in the deanery to organize a rota of volunteers to keep watch all day and all night to protect the building. Since the parish church could be the next target, I've come to ask you if you can organize the day watch and the night watch, two men at a time.'

'What a terrible thing, Vicar,' he said, frowning heavily. 'Yes, of course I'll get a rota going.'

'As far as tonight is concerned,' I suggested, 'I'll take over on my own and the verger can be responsible after Matins. Then perhaps tomorrow you can call a meeting of sidesmen and others to organize a proper rota.'

'As far as tonight is concerned, Vicar, I'll join you,' he said. 'We've got a camp bed up in the loft. I'll bring that with me when I come, so one of us can have a kip while the other keeps watch. Mind, how long this fire-watching will keep going will be a problem. You can't expect the men to do it for months on end.'

'Let's hope the police find the culprit as soon as possible,' I replied.

My wife was scathing when she came home for lunch, especially when I told her that I would be on duty that night. 'You need all the sleep you can get, without wasting those precious hours on a pointless exercise. And I'll tell you something else. Those volunteers will soon get tired of this potty business.'

'As soon as the law catches up with the perpetrator,' I said, 'then this potty business will be over, but for the time being we have to be on our guard.'

At about nine o'clock that evening, I went across to the church, armed with my old cricket bat and carrying a shopping bag containing a thermos flask of coffee and a packet of sandwiches. Joe Williams, our newly appointed verger, met me at the vestry door. 'I don't know 'ow long we've got to do this,' he remarked, 'but I've 'ad enough already.'

'Don't worry, Joe,' I replied, 'they'll soon catch him.'

Tom Beynon arrived with his camp bed and a pair of blankets at half past ten. 'I think you had better have a sleep first,' I suggested. 'Put the bed in the vestry and I'll read my book in my stall in the chancel.'

Apart from one alarm when a gust of wind banged a door in the church tower, the night passed uneventfully. 'Well, that's one night over safely,' said Tom.

The telephone was ringing when I went back to the Vicarage, still half asleep. It was the Superintendent. 'I told you it would happen. The parish church at Llanybedw has been burned to the ground.'

## 2

'How wrong can you be!' moaned Uncle Will when I phoned him later that morning. 'I thought it was sufficient to lock up the church. I went to bed at half past ten last night, positive that no harm would come to St Deiniol's. At five o'clock in the morning there was some almighty banging on the front door, as well as constant pressure on the doorbell. Margaret and I were in deep sleep. I put on my dressing gown and ran downstairs two at a time. Who should be on the doorstep but Jack the Trap, the biggest poacher in the village. He must have been out on one of his night raids.

'"Vicar, your church is on fire. There are flames coming from the roof, from everywhere as far as I can see." I rang the fire brigade, put on my overcoat over my pyjamas and dashed out. I had only gone a few yards down the drive and I could see the sky lit up in the distance. I don't know why they built the Vicarage so far from the church. At least I would have had some warning if it were next door to the building, like yours. By the time the fire brigade came it was too late to prevent the blaze spreading. They say it was started in the organ and that petrol had been used in large quantities. The only consolation is that the church silver and the registers were locked away in the safe in the vestry.

'Superintendent Brian Williams was doing his "What did I tell the Rural Dean?" routine. "It's not his fault," I told him. "He told everybody to keep a watch. Like most of the other incumbents I thought it was a waste of time." Apparently it was a dry, very windy night, ideal for an arsonist, whoever he may be.'

'I'll be round to see you this afternoon, Will. If it's any consolation to you about your ignoring of the Super-intendent's instructions, my wife was just as scathing about the need for fire-watching as you were. She even used your expression – "rubbish". I don't know whether he had some inside information or not, but I must admit that he was certainly on the ball.'

When Eleanor came in for lunch, she too suggested that perhaps the Superintendent had some inside information.

'In the first place,' she said, 'why should the Super-intendent of all people be up at an ecclesiastical prefab like St David's? I should have thought that one of his minions would have been sufficient to survey the damage. And why should he have been so positive about further attacks on our churches, even to the extent of suggesting that petrol would be used to burn the building? It sounds very suspicious to me.'

'Apparently he happened to be at the station when the news came in,' I replied. 'That's what Joe Trengrove, PC Plod, told Hugh, but it still doesn't explain his personal involvement.' Before going to the Vicarage at Llanybedw I went to see the parish church. It was a twelfth-century building with a square bell tower and, in the nave, a rood screen dating from the fifteenth century. The tower stood imperiously looking down upon the pile of smoking timber contained within the stone walls of the nave and chancel. In that pile were the cremated remains of the rood screen. It was a sickening sight.

I had never seen Will Evans so devastated. He looked as if he had suffered a family bereavement.

'I loved that church, Fred.' He spoke in muted tones. 'For the past twenty-two years I have celebrated the sacraments and preached the word in those lovely surroundings. I intended to stay here until my retirement in ten years' time. I suppose our dear Archdeacon will tell me what a challenge it will be to restore the church to its former glory. What can replace that ancient rood screen or those carved pews in the chancel? It will be a great opportunity for some young go-getter to make a name for himself. I can't face all the sweat and toil involved in the restoration.'

'What am I going to do if you leave the deanery, Will?' I said plaintively. 'You are my strong right arm.'

'Mr Rural Dean,' he replied, 'it is time that you learned to stand on your own two feet.'

Margaret Evans came into the study with a tray containing two cups of coffee and a plate of biscuits. 'Terrible, isn't it?' she said to me. 'Who would do a thing like that? The Superintendent was here this morning. He said he expected the person responsible to try it again before long, after he had been lying low for a while. It seems that he has a line of inquiry, as he put it, and that detectives will be working on it.'

'Typical of Brian Williams,' snorted Will, 'giving the impression that he knows everything!'

'Well, at least he did know enough to have prevented last night's disaster happening,' I replied.

'True enough, Fred,' he said, 'but whether that was just a guess on his part or not, it's difficult to say.'

'Anyway, Will,' I went on, 'I think I had better have a word with him to find out whether he knows more than he has been prepared to tell us.'

The next morning I telephoned the police station and asked to speak to Superintendent Williams. I arranged to meet him that afternoon at his office. I was ushered into a small room, dominated by a large desk behind which was seated the senior officer. He rose to greet me when I came in and we shook hands across the desk. 'Sit down, Mr Rural Dean,' he said, evidently trying to impress me with his *savoir faire*. He was a tall, thin man whose sparse grey hair had been combed across his balding head. A pair of rimless spectacles surmounted his beaky nose.

'I expect you want to know why I asked you to alert the parishes in your deanery to the danger of arson attacks on their churches,' he began, 'and why my request went unheeded at Llanybedw, with the subsequent disastrous result.'

'I must admit, Superintendent,' I replied, 'that I was somewhat puzzled why vandalism on my temporary church on the Brynfelin estate should warrant all-night vigils in every church in the deanery.'

'Well, in the first place,' he went on, 'what alarmed me was when my officers informed me that a hatchet must have been used to destroy the wooden altar cross. This was not the work of children, but the deliberate destruction of a Christian symbol by someone with a grudge against Christianity. Furthermore, it must have been done by a person who has been inside your church, possibly someone living on the estate.

'Now then, you can't destroy a brass cross but you can burn down the building which contains it. That was the next step. I felt that the ferocity which had prompted the attack on the wooden cross in St David's would impel this fanatic to vent his spleen elsewhere. What better than Llanybedw Church, out in the wilds where no one would expect such an outrage? Tomorrow we shall begin to conduct door-to-door enquiries on the estate. If any of your parishioners could contribute any information about someone who has extreme views on the Church or Christianity in general, let me know at once.'

Since the last thing that would be a topic of conversation on the estate would be the Christian religion, I felt that he was clutching at straws. However, I promised him that I would let him know immediately if I heard anything.

'In the meanwhile, insist that every church keeps a watch by day and night, Mr Rural Dean. That's all we can do at present.'

When I told my wife of the conversation over our evening meal, she said, 'I am most impressed. The police mandarin has decided that the person who vandalized St David's must have been someone living on the estate who knew that there was a wooden cross in the church. From that premise he goes on to predict that the suspect will wage war on all the churches in the deanery. Brilliant!'

'As I told Uncle Will,' I replied, 'you must admit that he has been uncannily accurate.'

'This is what worries me,' she retorted. 'Why Llanybedw? Will Evans told you that the Superintendent was a parishioner of his before he moved into the more affluent land of the *nouveaux riches* in Abergelly. From what he says, Brian Williams was not one of his favourite members of his flock. Suppose he is a closet Satanist?'

'Now you really are pushing the boat out!' I exploded. 'First of all, you told me that the idea of any further attacks on churches in the deanery was rubbish after the vandalism in St David's. Now you are indulging in rubbish of the kind which belongs to the comic-strip adventures of a Dan Dare. For someone who is a highly intelligent person, all I can assume is that you are suffering from some kind of mental delusion.'

She bridled at any suggestion which impinged on her medical integrity. 'Frederick Thomas Secombe, how dare you imply that my opinions are only fit for a children's comic! I only hope that you will not have to eat your words as I did mine.'

'How on earth can you suggest that someone dedicated to destroying churches would put every incumbent on the alert with all-night vigils and the like?' I asked. 'Not only that, but he is going to get his officers to make house-to-house enquiries on the estate.'

'That could be just a smoke-screen,' she said. 'Maybe the Satanism bit is an exaggeration, but you must admit that there is something very odd about his uncanny prediction.'

'All I can say is that it was either what you might term an educated guess on his part or that he has some inside information that he is not prepared to let us have,' I replied. 'If he is the know-all that Will Evans says he is, then that might explain it. In that case, he is failing in his duty just to pander to his own vanity. Perhaps I should have asked him point blank if he had been given some kind of tip-off. Anyway, in the meanwhile we must all be on our guard. I had a completely different reaction when I phoned around the deanery this morning. Everybody is organizing rotas of ecclesiastical fire-watches.'

'By the way, I am amazed that I have not heard from the Archdeacon,' I went on.

'Perhaps he is away somewhere,' said Eleanor. 'It is just as well. You have had enough to do without coping with his trinitarian venerableness.'

The Venerable Titus Phillips was a pompous cleric who had a curious habit of repeating every instruction in triplicate. He had not been well disposed towards me ever since he tripped over the folds of a voluminous tablecloth in the chancel of my church in Pontywen. The sight of his gaitered legs in the air as he lay on his back afforded great amusement to an audience of lay and clerical members who had come to his archidiaconal visitation. Ever since then I was *persona non grata* as far as he was concerned. This antipathy intensified when my fellow clergy elected me Rural Dean after the death of my predecessor. He had taken every opportunity of adding to my workload. I was prepared to receive a bombardment of telephone calls from him, implying some dereliction of duty on my part for the two attacks on the churches in my deanery.

The next morning the silence was explained when he rang me soon after I had arrived in the Vicarage after Matins. 'The Archdeacon here,' blasted the phone. 'I have just come back from a few days' holiday in Scotland to find out that two churches in your deanery have been, er, obliterated in the space of two days. I rang the Bishop but he says he has had no word from you. I would have thought that the first thing you would have done would be to inform his lordship of such serious happenings in the deanery.' I waited for the trinitarian formula to follow. 'The next time that anything like this happens, your immediate task must be to contact the Bishop. Let him know at once. You have a duty to tell him without fail when such catastrophic events occur.'

'Thank you for your advice, Mr Archdeacon,' I replied. 'All I can say in answer to that is that I was so concerned with asking all the incumbents in the deanery to organize the protection of their buildings, as requested by the police superintendent, that I forgot that I should have told his lordship about what had happened. May I correct you on one detail? Only one church has been obliterated. Our daughter church will be open for worship next Sunday. The small congregation have been magnificent under the leadership of their curate. They have repaired chairs and prayer books. One lady has been at work doing her best to minimize the damage to the altar frontal. Perhaps you would like to come to our Family Communion next Sunday and express your appreciation of what they have done.'

There was a silence at the other end of the phone, in contrast to the eruption which had begun the call. Then came a cough.

'I am, er, afraid that I shall be, er, unable to come. I have to dedicate an altar in a lady chapel at Cwmllynfi that morning. Perhaps I can come at a later date.'

'I am sure the congregation will look forward to that,' I replied. 'In the meantime, let us hope that this is the end of these frightful incidents in our deanery. I shall ring the

Bishop immediately after this conversation.' I put the phone down, then dialled the Bishop's palace. I was answered by the Bishop's secretary, an elderly lady who had befriended me when I appeared on his doorstep as a timid candidate for holy orders some twenty years before.

'Hello, Vicar,' she said cordially. 'I'm afraid the Bishop is not here at the moment. However, I shall tell him you have phoned. Sorry to hear about your troubles in the deanery; so is his lordship. I am sure he will want a word with you later. Are you keeping well?' Evidently there was no ill will at the episcopal headquarters.

No sooner had I put the phone down for the second time than there was a ring on the front doorbell. Our housekeeper had gone out to do the morning shopping. I sighed and made my way to answer the caller. I was confronted by a little man in a Harold Wilson trench coat, squinting at me through a pair of rimless spectacles. My heart dropped. It was Ed Jenkins, the local reporter for the evening newspaper. He had a habit of distorting everything I said in his zeal to promote an increased circulation for his editor.

'Sorry to call unannounced,' he squeaked in his high-pitched tones. 'I rang you earlier but you were engaged. I wondered if I could have a few words with you about this onslaught on the churches in your deanery.'

'I should hardly call it an onslaught, Mr Jenkins,' I replied. 'Our daughter church on the Brynfelin estate will be open for worship next Sunday. The only other church involved in an arson attack is at Llanybedw. There are twenty-two other churches unaffected. Anyway, I think you had better come in.'

He wiped his feet several times on the Vicarage doormat.

It was quite a sunny morning. We had not seen rain for several days. He followed me into my study, examined the cushions in the armchair, with which he must have been quite familiar since he had sat on them on numerous occasions, and then perched himself on the edge of them with his notebook in hand, his pencil poised.

'Now then, Vicar,' he began. 'I wonder if you could let me know whether you have any indication about the purpose of these two attacks on the, er, places of worship. Is it mindless vandalism or is there some more serious motive involved, such as might be a grudge against the Church in general, or in particular, perhaps?' He peered at me as if his stare could elicit a potential headline.

'At the moment,' I replied, 'the police have an open mind about the motive for these incidents. They are beginning house-to-house enquiries on the Brynfelin housing estate at this very moment.'

'I know that,' he said. 'Superintendent Williams told me this morning. Apart from that he told me nothing.'

'In that case, Mr Jenkins,' I replied, 'why on earth do you expect me to give you any further information?'

'I thought perhaps you might have your own ideas about what is happening.' He sounded disappointed. Then he tried another line of questioning. 'I suppose, as Rural Dean, you have warned all the churches in the deanery about further possible attacks?'

'I have indeed,' I said. 'In fact, they are all organizing 24-hour watches to prevent the arsonist from striking again. Here in the parish church the people's warden and I did an all-night watch. The pity is that there wasn't one at Llanybedw.'

His pencil worked furiously at this. I wished I had bitten my tongue. I could see poor Uncle Will being pilloried in the next edition of the newspaper.

'I suppose he thought it was sufficient to have the church securely locked,' I went on. 'No blame can be attached to the Vicar for what happened. Who would have thought that a church out in the country like Llanybedw would be the second place to follow the attack on a prefabricated building on a newly built housing estate in a town?'

He rattled his pencil between his dentures. 'I suppose,' he began again, 'there will be no services in your church at Brynfelin for the next few weeks at least.'

'On the contrary, Mr Jenkins,' I retorted, 'there will be services as usual next Sunday. The congregation may be small in numbers but under the leadership of the Curate, the Reverend Hugh Thomas, and Mr David Rees, the churchwarden, they have begun to repair the damage and there will be worship there on Sunday.'

'Excuse me, Vicar,' he said, 'by Mr David Rees you are referring to Dai Elbow, one of the most notorious offenders in Welsh rugby, whereas Hugh Thomas was one of the most promising outside halves we have had for some years until he abandoned his sporting career for the Church and his future marriage, if I may put it that way?'

'You may put it that way,' I replied. 'All I can say is that I never saw Mr Rees on the rugby field and I have only seen my curate once in a rugby jersey. Whatever their sporting background, I can assure you that they are both men whose reputation in the church at Brynfelin is impeccable. I am proud of them.'

He stood up and shook my hand. It was a limp hand-shake but a landmark in our relationship. He had never displayed such an attempt at cordiality since he had first appeared on my doorstep.

When Eleanor came in at lunchtime, I gave her the usual rundown of the events of the morning. 'Referring to the Archdeacon,' she said, 'I think it is about time we renamed him Pompous Titus rather than Trinitarian Rees. He really is a pain in the neck. As for Inquisitive Ed, I wonder why you were honoured with a handshake, even if it was of the token variety. Perhaps it was because he admired your con-version of a sinner into Saint David of Brynfelin.

'Now then, I have some news for you. Patients have been telling me about the door-to-door canvassing by the detectives. They are asking about neighbours who may have a car. As you know, there are not many car owners on the estate. Another question is about anybody who might have strong views of an atheistic kind. I would have thought that such persons would be very thin on the ground in that part of the world. Anyway, none of my customers knew anyone of that category. Indeed, one or two thought that atheism was some kind of new religion – so I don't think they will get very far with that line of enquiry. I am still suspicious about our Superintendent. All right, I am not accusing him of being responsible for the attacks, but his forecast of arson was too glib for me.'

'There's only one way to find out if he has unrevealed information,' I replied. 'I'll phone him this afternoon.'

'Why don't you go to see him?' she suggested.

For the second time in two days, I went to see the officer at the police station. 'Well, Mr Rural Dean,' he greeted me, relishing his use of the title, 'and what can I do for you?'

'It's more of a question of what you can do for me,' I said.

He raised his eyebrows. 'What do you mean?' he asked, somewhat nettled by the reversal of roles.

'Don't think this is an impertinence on my part, Superintendent,' I replied, with an emphasis on his title, 'but I have a feeling that you know something that I do not know. If so, I should be more than grateful if you would tell me what it is. I promise that I will not tell anybody else, but it would give me more of an incentive to make sure that all the churches in the deanery are on their guard.'

He looked me straight in the eye and did not speak for a few moments. 'You are very perceptive, Vicar. Yes, we have reason to believe that the person responsible for these attacks is a mentally deranged clergyman, the Reverend Herbert John Phillips. He was a curate in this deanery until three years ago, when he suffered a severe mental collapse. Since then he has been in and out of mental hospitals. He disappeared from Penyglais Mental Hospital a few weeks ago, where he had become physically aggressive.'

'I met him once, a year or so ago,' I interjected. 'He rang the doorbell fiercely. When my housekeeper answered it, he pushed her out of the way and burst into my study. After a few minutes of his weird gabbling, I said something which displeased him and he bolted from the house, running up the drive like a bat out of hell.'

The Superintendent seemed delighted at this piece of information. 'You know him, splendid!' he exclaimed. 'It may be that he will visit you again in the very near future.

If so, you must detain him under some pretext or other and phone us immediately. You see, recently, in the hospital, he had begun to rave about the Church, which he said had become the tool of Satan. As a result, when he escaped from Penyglais, they informed us that he was at large. So when we were told of the vandalism at St David's and I saw that wooden cross chopped to pieces, I felt sure that the Reverend Phillips was responsible and the attacks would continue. Mind you, I didn't think it would be the very next day.'

'Why didn't you tell me this at the outset?' I asked him.

'Well,' he replied, 'since we had no proof that he was responsible – and, indeed, neither have we now – our rules of procedure do not allow us to name names. All the more so in this case, since it involves a clergyman, of all people. So I did the best I could under the circumstances. What is worrying us at the moment is that we do not know where he is. Obviously he was in the vicinity of your church at Brynfelin at one time, otherwise he would not have known that you had a wooden cross. Wherever he was staying he must have had access to a hatchet. Apparently he does drive. However, we have had no report of any stolen car in the area. It seems he is a man of private means, with cash in his possession. That is why we have been trying to find out if he had been trying to get lodgings in one of the houses on the estate.

'Now you know all the information I have. I should be obliged if you would keep this to yourself, and in the meanwhile, should you have anything you think worthwhile, let us have it immediately.'

On my way back from the police station, I decided to call in at the church to check if the verger was on duty.

I had told him that under no circumstances was he to leave the doors unlocked. I went around to the vestry and was about to knock on the door when I realized it was slightly ajar. I pushed the door wide open and strode into the room. There was no sign of life in the vestry or any other part of the church. By now I was consumed with righteous indignation. It was like finding an empty sentry box outside Buckingham Palace. Back in the vestry I became aware of a faint smell of tobacco smoke floating in through the open door. I tiptoed around the side of the chancel to discover a nicotine cloudlet arising from behind a tombstone.

'This is a fine way of keeping watch!' I yelled. A bald head appeared over the top of Nicholas Evans' memorial, followed seconds later by the rest of its large supporting structure. It was not a pretty sight. The verger's face had not been touched by a razor for some days. His shirt had not been in the wash tub for a lot longer and was suffering from the strain of containing his beer belly, with the consequent loss of a couple of buttons. He was not repentant.

'Look, Vicar,' he growled, 'if you think I'm going to stay in there for hours on end, without a fag, you've 'ad it. I'm not paid to be a fire-watcher. In any case, I'm 'ardly getting a small fortune. 'Ow long do you think this business is going to go on? I tell you what, a few more days of this and I'm off.' I was not prepared for this insubordination, and stood speechless. Then my earlier yelling gave place to a quiet plea for his help.

'I'm sorry, Joe,' I murmured, 'but this is an emergency. I've got a rota of old age pensioners to come to relieve you during the daytime. In any case, with a bit of luck we'll have this man put away very shortly.'

'You 'ope,' he retorted, and went inside.

Eleanor was quite sympathetic to his attitude when I told her what had transpired.

'You can't expect the man to be giving up all his time to this business, with no end in sight,' she remarked as we were having our evening meal.

'I have something else to tell you in private later on,' I said. 'It is very confidential.'

'I can't wait,' she replied.

When the children had gone to bed and Mrs Cooper was in her room, I gave her a detailed account of my conversation with the Superintendent. 'My apologies to the top sleuth,' she said, when I had finished my resumé of his information. 'It was so obvious that there was more to the incident at St David's than what we had been told. But there is one thing that puzzles me about all this. Where has this mad parson been hiding? Has he been in a cave somewhere? In that case he would have been even more recognizable than John the Baptist. Where would he get the money to buy a hatchet and petrol and all the other accompaniments necessary for his foul deeds?'

'He comes from a wealthy family,' I replied. 'His father was an industrialist somewhere in the Midlands. I would think that he would have access to more than enough money to finance his Satanic endeavours.'

Our tête-à-tête was interrupted by the ring of the telephone. 'Don't say this is news of number three,' said my wife.

When I picked up the receiver there was some heavy breathing at the other end. 'Don't think this is the finish of your troubles.' The voice was immediately recognizable.

# 3

I stood by my desk, the phone shaking in my hand. Before I could reply to what I assumed came from a call box, there was a click at the other end. The mad arsonist had said his piece and departed. When I returned my wife said, 'That was a very short conversation. A wrong number, I suppose?'

'Oh no!' I replied vehemently. 'The caller had the right number all right. He spoke just one sentence and then rang off. It was the Reverend Herbert Phillips. He informed me that I was not to think that this was the finish of my troubles.'

'Sit down, love,' she ordered, 'and swallow what's left of your whisky. That will bring back the colour to your cheeks. When you have settled down you had better ring the police straight away.'

Ten minutes later I rang the police station and asked to speak to Superintendent Brian Williams, saying it was urgent. After what seemed an interminable wait, he announced his presence. 'Have you any information you can give us, Mr Rural Dean?' he asked.

'I have just had a phone call from the suspect, who told me that I was not to think my troubles had finished. Then the phone was put down. There was such menace in his voice that I felt that a gun had been pointed at my head.'

There was a pause. 'Did the call come from a call box?' he asked.

'I think so,' I replied. 'I thought I could hear some traffic noise in the background.'

'Tomorrow we shall have to intensify our enquiries,' he said. 'I am speaking from home at the moment. There's nothing more can be done tonight. As far as you are concerned, Mr Rural Dean, you had better put all your parishes on special alert tomorrow morning. Don't worry. You sound as if you have been shaken by the phone call. We'll get this madman. Somebody somewhere must know where he is.'

When I told Eleanor this, she said, 'Does this somebody know what he has been doing? If so, there must be two anti-clerical nuts at large.'

'I hardly think so,' I replied. 'It is more likely that some old dear is providing him with bed and breakfast, little knowing that she is harbouring a viper in her bosom.'

'That's very Shakespearean,' commented my wife. 'All the police have to do is to look for Mrs Cleopatra Jones in the telephone directory and they've got him!'

'It's no laughing matter, Eleanor,' I said peevishly. 'Until this man is caught every church in the deanery is in danger of obliteration.'

'I'm sorry, love,' she replied, and put her arm around me. 'I know this is a very serious situation. You must forgive my feeble attempt to ease the burden upon you, Mr Rural Dean. Perhaps a better solution would be a good night's rest with the aid of a dose of aspirins. The combination of the Scotch and the pills should ensure the necessary slumber.'

She was right. The next morning I awoke to a new day and a determination to do all I could to help the police find the Reverend Herbert John Phillips. I went across to the church for Matins, where I found Tom Beynon and Rhys Griffiths coming off the night shift to be replaced by a disgruntled Joe Williams. We were joined by Hugh Thomas, who had been holding the fort at St David's with Dai Elbow. Immediately I found myself embroiled in a welter of discontent about the need for a 24-hour watch in the churches.

'Before you say anything else,' I bellowed above the confusion of noise in the vestry, 'I think you should know that I had a phone call from the arsonist last night, informing me that I must not think that my troubles were finished. If you could have heard the intensity of the threat in that man's voice, you would realize the need for the utmost vigilance in protecting our churches.'

There was an instant silence. Tom Beynon was the first to speak. 'In that case, that's it for the time being', he pronounced, like a judge announcing a verdict. 'There's no alternative but to keep a watch on our buildings. The only thing, Vicar, is that there is a limit to that. You take it, I am not going to work until the two till ten shift, but Rhys here is due at the office at nine o'clock. It's now nearly eight o'clock and he's got to get home, wash, shave and have his breakfast, then cycle ten minutes to the Blaenwern estate to be there by nine o'clock. You've got the Curate here, who has been up all night at St David's and who looks half asleep, if he doesn't mind me saying so

– how can you expect him to be on his toes in the parish for the rest of today?'

It was now my turn to be silent. 'All I can say in answer to that, Tom,' I replied, 'is that I hope the Wisdom of Solomon is granted to Superintendent Brian Williams and his men to enable them to catch this man before he can do any more damage. They will be scouring every bed and breakfast place in the district. In the meanwhile, all the churches in the deanery must be on the alert.'

Tom and Rhys Griffiths departed. The verger went out into the churchyard to enjoy a few cigarettes while I and a very tired curate said Matins. To say that Hugh's contribution to the service was mumbled would be an understatement. It was a very relieved young man who was told by his vicar that he should go to bed and take the rest of the day off.

By the time I had finished ringing around the deanery with the instruction from the Superintendent that every parish should be on its guard, it was eleven o'clock. I decided to turn my attention to my sermon preparation for the Sunday. This involved a perusal of the collect, epistle and gospel for the day as a first step. If the Church had chosen pieces of Scripture for each Sunday, I thought that I had the obligation to expand them. As I was preening my feathers at my devotion to the prayer book, I became aware that there was little in the appointed lessons to stimulate a worthwhile sermon. Then I recalled the advice given to a young curate who had gone to the great nineteenth-century historian Bishop Stubbs to ask for guidance in preaching. 'Preach about God and preach about twenty minutes,' said the prelate. 'Good morning, and please close the door as you go out!'

This led me to think about the renegade arsonist and his feud with God. Surely here was a theme which would be more relevant to the situation facing us in Abergelly than anything in the appointed readings for the Sunday. I decided to break with my long-cherished custom and preach about the recent happenings in the neighbourhood.

As I sat ruminating at my desk, I was startled by the ring of the phone, which was in close proximity to my right ear. I picked up the receiver with a shaking hand, praying that the caller would not be the subject for next Sunday's sermon. To my great relief I heard the unmistakable voice of Superintendent Brian Williams. To my much greater relief I heard him say in triumphal tones, 'Mr Rural Dean, we've got him!'

'Hooray!' I shouted.

'Acting on a hunch,' he went on, 'I instructed one of my detectives to do a tour of the garages in the district to enquire if any suspicious person had come in to purchase a can of petrol. At 10.35 he rang me to say that an unshaven man in scruffy clothing had only just left the Park End Garage on the Pontywen Road, carrying a can of petrol. Apparently he had been sleeping rough ever since he left the hospital. He had plenty of money on him, but obviously had avoided lodging anywhere in case he might be traced there. I shall give you more details once we have finished questioning him. The great thing is, Mr Rural Dean, that you and your fellow clergy can rest in peace.'

'Thank you very much, Superintendent,' I replied. 'I shall have the utmost pleasure in ringing all the incumbents in the deanery to let them know the glad tidings.

Less than an hour ago I was warning them to be on their guard. The Lord has been gracious unto Sion.'

'With the help of Detective Constable Protheroe,' added the Superintendent.

There was a paean of praise for the Abergelly police from the whole of the deanery. Those incumbents whose inertia had been disturbed by the necessity of fire-watching could now go back to their slumbering priest-hood, while those whose care of their parishioners was more energetic could return to activities unencumbered by the threat of arson in their churches. The one exception to this chorus of appreciation was supplied by my wife when she came home from her duties as a general practitioner at lunchtime. As soon as she came through the door I rushed to meet her with the joyful news.

'Thank God for that!' she said. 'I must say that your Superintendent was quick on the draw. How did they trace the culprit?'

'Well,' I replied, 'according to the Superintendent, this morning he had a hunch that if his minions visited all the garages in the district to enquire if anybody had been in to buy a can of petrol, it would give them a lead. As it happened the arsonist had been in the Park End Garage just a few minutes previously, and a squad car picked him up.'

'Hold on,' said Eleanor. 'It was not until this morning that our sleuth had the idea of doing the rounds of all the garages to find out if there had been any purchase of cans of petrol?'

'That's right,' I replied.

'I retract my statement that he was quick on the draw,' she said. 'Since it was obvious that poor old Uncle Will's

39

church at Llanybedw was destroyed by the use of petrol, why on earth did he not instigate his investigation of petrol stations until this morning? It seems to me that his hunch, as he calls it, suffers from an impediment in its gestation. He could even have begun an investigation before that, when St David's was attacked. If you remember, he said that next time a church was attacked, it would not be wine which would be sprinkled around, but petrol, and where do you get petrol? I'm sorry, Fred, but after due consideration, I'm afraid he does not get brownie points from me. However, the one thing that matters most to me, my dear, is that a big load has been lifted from your shoulders. If this threat to the deanery had continued, you would have been a shadow of your former self in no time.' She pecked me on my cheek and said, '*Bon appetit*' as we tucked into Mrs Cooper's snack of liver and onions.

After we had finished our meal, my wife asked, 'Have you informed the Bishop that the dreaded miscreant has been apprehended?'

'I have not,' I replied. 'I have been too busy taking the weight off the minds of twenty-two incumbents. Nevertheless, at thy bidding, I shall inform my master that the deanery has been delivered from the hand of the enemy and that no more petrol will be sprinkled over the countless treasures of our ancient churches, as well as the not so ancient ones.'

'Sometimes, my dear Frederick,' she commented, 'I wonder why you wasted your sweetness on the desert air of the pulpit, instead of gambolling in the lush pastures of academia.'

'For the simple reason, my sweetheart, that there are no human beings in academia, just desiccated old sticks.'

'Language, Secombe!' she exclaimed. 'But how true.'

The Bishop received the news with relief but, typically, with sorrow that one of his clergy had fallen prey to dementia. 'Herbert Phillips has a fine intellect,' he said. ' "True genius is to madness near allied and thin partitions do their bounds divide." How sad that someone who could have been a beacon of scholarship in the Church should have become its dedicated enemy.'

After I rang his lordship, I thought I had better inform the Archdeacon that the arsonist had been arrested. 'Archdeacon here,' was the pompous reply when I dialled his number.

'Rural Dean here,' I said in a tone to match his. 'The Rural Dean of the Abergelly Deanery.' There was a silence while his venerableness strove to come to terms with this mockery. 'I am ringing to let you know that the threat to the churches has been ended by the arrest of the wanted man.' I waited for the inevitable question.

'Have you informed the Bishop?'

It was with great delight that I replied, 'I have indeed. He was greatly relieved to hear the news, as I am sure you must be, Mr Archdeacon.'

'Oh yes, yes, yes,' he stammered. 'When, er, did this happen?'

'At about eleven o'clock this morning,' I went on. 'He was arrested after purchasing a can of petrol from the Park End Garage here in Abergelly. Superintendent Williams says that he will let me have further details after the culprit has been further questioned. However, what matters most is that the attacks on the churches are now at an end. All the incumbents can go to bed tonight safe in the knowledge that nothing can happen to harm their churches.'

'Oh, yes, yes, yes,' he murmured. Then he added, 'I would suggest that at the next Chapter meeting, you had better get them to examine their insurance policies to see that they are fully covered for fire damage – fully covered. It is important that they are fully covered.'

My next move in the line of duty was to inform Tom Beynon that he could cancel his list of volunteer fire-watchers. He received the news with great joy.

'As I told you, Vicar,' he said, 'if this business had gone on for any length of time you would have had to scrape the barrel to get anybody. We can concentrate now on building up the numbers in the congregation. I've been thinking – how about forming a men's club? You know the sort of thing, meeting once a month in a pub rather than the church hall and getting a list of good speakers. Perhaps we could play a few games of cricket against some of the other churches in the district.'

'Fine, Tom,' I replied, 'if you are willing to organize the proceedings. We have to beware of having too many orga-nizations. That's the only snag. As you know, we are now rehearsing *The Mikado* with the G and S. Hugh Thomas has got a good youth club going in St David's, not to men-tion the Young Wives' Group Janet is hoping to start, as a potential young wife. Then of course, there's the Mothers' Union, not to mention Willie James' Boy Scouts, plus the old age pensioners' meeting in St David's. Yes, I think your men's club is an excellent idea as long as you don't expect me to run it.'

'Of course not, Vicar,' he said. 'I know what a work load you've got now with your Rural Dean's duties and all that, but as long as you give it your blessing, that's all I need.'

'You have that, Tom,' I replied warmly. 'We'll have to give it a title. I know, we have St Peter's key emblazoned on the wooden base which holds the altar cross. Why not call it "The Keys Club"?' So was born the Keys Club.

When I called around to see Dai Elbow, who was on the same six till two shift as Tom Beynon, I was greeted with a beaming smile.

'Well, I 'ear they've comprehended the criminal,' he announced.

'News travels fast!' I said. 'I was just coming to tell you that. Where did you get that information?'

'I met PC Watts when I was coming off the shift. That'll save a lot of trouble. We'd only got six to 'elp out at St David's – I was beginning to think that me and the Curate would have to sleep up there permanent like. Come on in, Vicar, and 'ave a glass of my rhubarb wine to celebrate.'

By the time I had drunk a second glass my head was beginning to spin. I had drunk two tumblers of whisky with Tom, who had persuaded me that a bottle of stout was no way to signal the end of the all-night vigils. It was fortunate for me that I had not used the car to make my visits. By the time I reached the Vicarage gates my legs were ceasing to co-operate. I was thankful that Eleanor had not returned from her afternoon stint at the hospital. It was with great difficulty that I managed to get my key into the lock of the front door. When eventually I managed to complete the exercise, I pushed the door forward and fell into the arms of Mrs Cooper, who had become aware of the fact that someone was tampering with the lock.

The housekeeper was a sturdy lady and held me up with no difficulty. 'Vicar!' she exclaimed. 'You've been having one more than the eight, as they say. If you go and sit yourself down in the study, I'll bring you a cup of strong coffee. That will sober you down by the time Dr Secombe comes home.'

She was right. By the time my wife arrived I had recovered my equilibrium, both mental and physical. The only fly in the ointment, if one could describe it as such, was the bottle of champagne she had bought 'to celebrate'. When I said, 'Oh no!' she looked at me quizzically.

'I see. You have already done that,' she murmured. 'I suggest we put it in the fridge until tomorrow's dinner.'

'I'm afraid my two wardens provided me with a mixture of rhubarb wine and whisky,' I replied, 'and when that comes in tumblerfuls, that's more than a man can stand.'

'Or stand up,' she added.

Next morning after Matins my curate asked if he could see me later in the Vicarage to discuss a private matter. We arranged to meet at eleven o'clock. When I told Eleanor, who was getting into her car to go to the surgery, she said, 'That sounds ominous. Tell me all when I come home for lunch.'

It was quite obvious as soon as he came into the study that something was weighing heavily on his mind. 'Sit down, Hugh,' I said. 'Would you like a cup of coffee before we begin our discussion?'

'If you don't mind, Vicar,' he replied, 'I think I would like to get this off my chest and have the coffee afterwards.'

'By all means,' I said. He took a deep breath and bounded into the reason for his visit.

'The Vicar of Waun y Llwn is advertising for a curate. There is a house with the curacy. It looks to me as if there will not be a house available on the estate for some time. Janet and I are desperate to get married. I am going to phone him when I leave here to arrange for an interview. Before I did that I wanted you to know what I intended doing.'

'Thank you for letting me know,' I said, 'but I would suggest that you hold your horses for a day or two. I shall get in touch with Alderman Stewart after you go, and explain that unless he can provide a house on Brynfelin in the very near future, I shall lose an excellent curate.'

'I think I'll have that coffee now, Vicar,' he replied. 'The last thing I want to do is leave you in the lurch with so much needing to be done. If the council can provide me with a house, I can tell you that I am prepared to stay for the nine years that are left to build a church on the estate.'

Half an hour later I rang the Alderman. 'I wonder if I can come and see you urgently on a matter of vital importance to the church at Brynfelin?' I asked.

'By all means, Vicar,' he said. 'In any case, I want to have a word with you on another subject. I've got to go out now, but I'll be back by about three o'clock this afternoon. Would that time suit you?'

'Splendid,' I replied.

'Why this sudden rush to get married?' speculated Eleanor when she came home for lunch. 'You don't think it's a shotgun wedding?'

'Of course not,' I said. 'Hugh is honest enough to have told me if that was the case. They are very much in love and can't wait indefinitely until a house is found for them. It's simply that.'

'Well let's hope that the dear Alderman can pull enough strings to get them their place. By the way, why does he want to have a word with you on another subject?' she enquired.

'I have a pretty good idea about that,' I replied. 'I think he is going to ask me to be his chaplain when he becomes Mayor next May.'

'Good gracious!' she said. 'You are going to be an important person. Rural Dean and Mayor's Chaplain! It's just as well that you decided not to buy a black hat with a black rosette on the headband. Your head is big enough as it is. It would be swollen even more by next May. Just playing!' she added, and kissed me.

At three o'clock I was sitting in the comfortably furnished front room of the Alderman's house, ensconced in a cut-moquette covered armchair, with a glass of whisky on the occasional table beside me.

'Well now, Vicar,' asked the Mayor-Elect, 'what can I do for you?'

'Let me put it this way,' I said, 'the one great need for the Church's work on the Brynfelin estate at the moment is a house for the Curate. Hugh Thomas is doing excellent work there, but is anxious to get married and settle down on the estate for these vital years before the permanent church is built. This morning he told me that because he can see no sign of a house becoming available up there, he was thinking of applying for a post in another parish where there is a parsonage. I remember you telling me at the time of the Earl of Duffryn's visit to the parish church, when you were present, that if there was anything you could do to further the Church's mission in Brynfelin, you would be only too pleased to do it. Now then, Alderman, please, please can you do anything to keep this young man in the parish? In other words, can you persuade the Housing Committee to find a place for him?'

He sat back in his armchair, reached for his tumbler of Scotch, took a generous helping and composed his large corporeal presence. 'From what you tell me, Vicar, it seems vital, vital that you hold on to this live wire.' He paused. 'I'll tell you what, I'll have a word with Ben Davies, the Housing Committee Chairman, at the council meeting tonight. I think you can take it for granted that we'll do something straight away. I'll give you a ring later tonight after the meeting.

'Now for my reason to speak with you. As you know, I am due to become Mayor next May and I shall need a chaplain. I'm afraid that I have not been to your church since the Earl of Duffryn came to St Peter's, what with one thing and another. However, I am not an irreligious man and I shall make an effort to come to a service occasionally. In other words, I should be more than delighted if you would be my chaplain for my term of office.' He spoke quite rapidly in his high-pitched, squeaky voice, running one sentence into another in a similar fashion to Ed Jenkins, the local reporter. The only difference between them was that Ed was a beanpole of a man and the Alderman was a short, rectangular tank.

'I shall be honoured to accept the position,' I replied. 'The one snag is that since I have been appointed Rural Dean, that is one more call upon my time in addition to

47

the demands that a busy parish entails. So within the constraints that those duties impose upon me, I shall do my best to be a conscientious chaplain.'

'All it entails, Vicar,' he went on, 'is that you have to say the prayers at every council meeting and preach at the service which follows the mayor-making, and that's about it. Since the council meetings are only once a month, it shouldn't be too much of a burden. Thank you very much. Let's drink to our time together, shall we?' He poured himself a full portion of whisky and topped up my glass. 'Here's to us,' he proclaimed and emptied the Scotch in one gulp, to my astonishment.

It took me half an hour to finish my drink, in which time he managed to consume another libation. He stood up to bid me farewell without a sign of imbalance. As I recalled my collapse into my housekeeper's arms the previous day, I marvelled at his capacity to hold his liquor.

'It looks as if Hugh will have his house,' I told Eleanor when she came in from her visiting. 'Our friend the Alderman says I can take it for granted that something will be done straight away after he has had a word with the Chairman of the Housing Committee.'

'Wait and see, love,' she advised. 'Let's hope that the phone call tonight will deliver the goods. For heaven's sake, don't tell Hugh tonight at the rehearsal that the house is in the bag, if you will pardon the mixed metaphor. Just tell him that you have been to see the big man and that perhaps you will have good news when he comes to Matins tomorrow.'

The rehearsal that night was the last one before my wife began her stint as stage director. Hugh's tenor voice had developed considerably during the music sessions of the past three months. Graham Webb was a gifted tutor. He had taught my curate how to sing from his chest instead of his throat. I blessed the day that Ivor Hodges had suggested that his music master would make an ideal maestro for our infant Gilbert and Sullivan Society, especially since he had now a dual role as parish organist and choirmaster.

My curate was heartened by the prospect that I might have good tidings for him in the morning. He had promised in his interview with me earlier that he would sing Nanki-Poo before he left the parish.

'So it may not be my swan song,' he said excitedly.

'Now hold on, young man,' I warned him. 'Wait until tomorrow.'

The musical director congratulated him at the end of rehearsal. 'I don't know what has happened to you,' he remarked, 'but you have never sung so freely and wholeheartedly as you have this evening. Sing like that when it comes to the performance and you will bring the house down.' Coming from Graham, that was praise indeed.

At ten o'clock that evening, the phone rang. I deserted the television programme we were watching in the sitting room and dashed to answer the call in my study.

'You can tell your curate that he can get married as soon as he likes' were the opening words from the Alderman.

'Wonderful!' I exclaimed.

'A couple are moving out of a house in Hillside Crescent. The husband has got a job in the Ford factory in Swansea. The housing manager says the place is in excellent condition. There is one proviso, and that is that they must move in as soon as possible. By the way, I have told the Council that you will be my chaplain, so you can expect a visit from Ed Jenkins tomorrow. Sorry to ring so late, but I thought you would like to have the news tonight to put you out of your anxiety.'

'Thank you so much, Alderman,' I replied. 'You could have rung me after midnight with that kind of information. It will be a delighted young man who will hear what I have to tell him in church tomorrow morning.'

I came back to the sitting room, and before I could say anything Eleanor came to me and put her arms around me. 'You don't need to tell me, Frederick,' she said. 'The Lord has been gracious unto you for the second time in three days.'

'Apparently,' I replied. 'A couple are moving out of a well-kept house to go to Swansea. The one proviso is that Hugh and Janet must move in as soon as possible. From what he was saying to me, that will be no trouble at all.'

'There's just one snag,' commented my wife. 'What are they going to do about furniture?'

'He must have thought about that,' I said. 'His parents are comfortably off. I expect Janet has some money by her. She is earning a fair amount from her job at the council offices and does not have to pay for lodgings, since she is at home with her parents. I can see a wedding at St Peter's within the next six weeks!'

# 4

When I told my curate that a council house in good condition was available for occupation as long as there was no delay in the tenancy, his joy was unbounded. 'You can call our banns next Sunday, Vicar,' he said.

'More importantly, Hugh,' I replied, 'will you be able to furnish the house in such a short space of time?'

'Don't worry,' he went on, 'that has all been seen to. Our bedroom suite has been purchased and is waiting for delivery in Harris's store in Cardiff, and there is a three-piece suite my parents are giving us in store in Abergavenny. As for the kitchen furniture and so on, we can go down to Cardiff to order that some time this week. It will be a quiet wedding. There's no point in spending money on an elaborate affair with a multitude of guests and expensive wedding gowns. Janet is going to wear a smart two-piece costume which she can use for best after the ceremony, and her two friends who will be brides-maids already have their dresses. That's it! I have asked David Parry, my college friend, to be my best man. There will be no formal dress.'

'Hugh!' I said. 'You never cease to amaze me. I expect you have chosen the hymns and the wedding music.'

'We have indeed,' he replied. 'I'll have a word with Graham Webb at the G and S rehearsal on Wednesday. That's another thing. We have decided to have only a week off for our honeymoon, so that won't interfere very much with the *Mikado* rehearsals. Dr Secombe will be pleased about that, I'm sure.'

I caught Eleanor on the doorstep as she was about to get into her car to drive to her surgery. 'If you don't mind, love,' I said, 'I think you had better come back inside before you drive off.'

'Well, make it snappy,' she replied. I gave her a summary of what I had been told, including the reference to the *Mikado* rehearsals. 'I'll tell you something, Frederick,' she commented, 'if that offer of a council house had not come so quickly, you would have lost a very good curate. Obviously everything had been arranged for an immediate wedding. So I shall have a clerical neighbour up in Brynfelin. Good show!' With that she was back in her car and did her usual Brands Hatch exit through the Vicarage gates.

Halfway through the *Times* crossword, I was disturbed by the ring of the telephone. It was the squeaky voice of Ed Jenkins.

'Congratulations, Vicar. I hear you are to be the Mayor's Chaplain next May. I wonder if I might call round to see you about the appointment and also to get your reaction to the arrest of the suspect for the arson attacks on the churches in your deanery?' He did not pause for breath. His lungs must have been in good order despite his addiction to tobacco.

'By all means, Mr Jenkins,' I said. 'How soon do you want this interview?'

'In an hour's time, say?' came the reply.

I still had two clues left in the crossword and a half-written letter to my parents lying on the desk when the protracted pressure on the button of the doorbell brought Mrs Cooper making her unhurried way to the front door, complaining about the perpetrator. She poked her head around the study door, after waiting for me to answer her knock. 'It's that man from the paper,' she announced in aggrieved tones. 'Why he's got to make such a hell of a balloo I don't know. I can hear that noise from three streets away, as they do say.'

With that piece of poetry she went back to the doorstep and then ushered the reporter into the study. He sat at the other side of the desk from me, produced a pencil and notebook from his jacket, leaned back in his chair, adjusted his spectacles, cleared his throat and began his questioning in his high-pitched, nasal tones.

'Well now, Vicar, as I said over the phone, congratulations on your appointment. I must say that you will have an excellent Mayor in Alderman Walters, a man of honesty, much respected after he unleashed that can of worms about corruption in the Highways Department a few years ago. If you don't mind me saying so, I wonder how such a busy person as yourself is going to cope with being Rural Dean and Vicar of a demanding parish and now, before long, with all the duties of Mayor's Chaplain?'

'In answer to that, Mr Jenkins,' I replied, 'the Mayor has assured me that apart from saying prayers to begin the monthly council meetings and a few ceremonial occasions during his year of office, there will be little else to do. He knows all about my commitments and is anxious to see that they are not affected by the chaplaincy.'

'Well, I'm glad about that, because the Reverend William Protheroe has been out and about wherever the present Mayor goes, like Mary's little lamb. But there, how much work has he got to do as minister of one of the five Baptist churches in the town, and I think his must be the smallest.'

He paused in his 'interview'. 'Now then, Mr Rural Dean, using your other hat, as it were, what information can you give me about the arrest of the suspect in connection with the arson attacks on the churches in your deanery?' He peered at me over his spectacles, which had slipped down his nose and seemed to be in danger of falling off.

'In the first place, Mr Jenkins,' I said testily, 'there has been only one arson attack. The desecration of St David's at Brynfelin did not involve arson. I think the police are to be congratulated on making such an early arrest. It means that all the incumbents in the deanery can now end their fire-watching efforts and can concentrate on their parochial duties. Second, I am not allowed to divulge any information about the suspect because he is still being questioned in Abergelly Police Station. Until he is charged with the offence, I cannot name the person.'

'You know him then?' came the reply. 'You see, there are rumours going around that the man is a deranged cleric.'

I realized that I had made a big mistake by saying that I could not name the person. Ed Jenkins was too well versed in the way of eliciting information to miss the opportunity of exploiting my slip of the tongue. I had suffered from his perspicuity in this respect too often in the past.

'Look, Mr Jenkins,' I said huffily, 'I did not say that I knew the suspect. All I told you was that I was not allowed to name the person.'

'Let me put it this way,' he replied, 'if the culprit was a tramp or somebody like that, there would be no point in naming the person. I doubt if you would even know his name – why should you? – but you gave the impression that you knew the man involved. My apologies, Vicar, if I upset you. I think I had better go before I annoy you any further. I promise that I shall not say in my report that you know the suspect.'

He stood up, did not attempt to shake my hand, and told me that he would see himself out. It was obvious that he had got what he wanted.

I waited for Eleanor to tell me that I was an innocent abroad when she came home for lunch. To my surprise, she said, 'My dear love, you told Ed the news-hound the truth, that you could not name the person. If he cared to put his own interpretation on that statement it was up to him. In any case, he cannot print the name of the mad person. More to the point is the fact that somebody has got hold of the identity of the arsonist, and come what may, before long most of the population of Abergelly will know that poor old Herbert John Phillips is the culprit. You know what this place is like.

'I am much more interested in what Hugh Thomas told you. I shall be paying a visit to Howell's in Cardiff to purchase a new costume for the occasion. By the way, you could do with a new suit from Wippell's, your clerical outfitter. I think it is about time that you had a grey suit instead of that perpetual black stuff you always wear. It will look much better when you come to perform your chaplaincy duties.'

When the first stage rehearsal of *The Mikado* arrived later in the week with my wife in her new role as director, the Curate was irrepressible, so much so that she had to remind him that he was not playing the Major-General, the comic in the last opera, but Nanki-Poo, the romantic lead.

'My apologies, Madam Director,' he said. 'I am still a little light-headed after hearing the glad tidings that I am to be married in six weeks' time and that Janet and I will be among the folk who live on the hill.'

'All I can tell you, Hugh, as one who works among those who live on the hill,' she replied, 'is that your delirium of excitement will fade away quite quickly when you get there as a resident.'

'In answer to that,' he said, 'don't forget that my wife-to-be has lived there for the past six years without any grave danger to her health, and that she has been very happy there.'

'As Vicar of this parish and the Koko of this production, might I suggest that we end this dialogue and move on to the entrance of the Lord High Executioner, which is the next item to be rehearsed according to your schedule pinned up on the kitchen door this morning?'

My intervention was greeted with a broad grin by Nanki-Poo and with a withering glance from my wife, one of her specials. 'Who is producing this show?' she demanded.

'You are, Madam Director,' I replied, 'and very competently indeed for a first rehearsal, if I may say so.'

'You may say so,' she said sharply, 'and for God's sake don't be so condescending. Right, everybody. Now then, gentlemen, up on stage for your entrance, tenors on the right and basses on the left. You come on in single file, you will have fans, which will be closed, and once you are in place you begin your chorus. On the first word, 'Behold', you point with the closed fan at centre back stage, where the Lord High Executioner will appear. Now, don't forget that you are nobles. Taking your time from the music, you step in lordly fashion, heads held high, shoulders back, something like Japanese Welsh Guards.'

As the members of the Abergelly Male Voice Chorus plus a few male members of the congregation scrambled on to the stage, my wife followed them up the steps in sprightly fashion.

'Now then, sort yourselves out, everybody. The taller men to the back of the line, please. Hold on, I'll see to you.'

She spent the next ten minutes lining up the raw material which would occupy her attention for the next four months or so.

'Now then, Graham, we are ready, I think,' she informed the MD. He tapped his music stand and turned to Elwyn Gorman, the pianist. Elwyn was a shy, large young man whom I had persuaded to join the Society after his mother had suggested that it would do him good to meet people. 'Our Elwyn is an LRAM but spends all his time in the front room at the piano. As soon as he comes home from the office and has his dinner, it's straight into the front room and there he stays for the rest of the night.'

Graham Webb had been impressed by his musical ability but less impressed by his alertness at the piano. Elwyn seemed to be in a perpetual daydream. So it was now. The tap on the music stand had fallen on deaf ears.

'Elwyn!' he shouted. The pianist started up as if roused from the dead. 'The Chorus of Nobles on page 23.' There was a fumbling of the score.

'Got it, Graham,' he said eventually. The musical director gritted his teeth and then counted, 'One, two, three.' By the time the problem of co-ordination of movement, actions and music had been faced by the stage director, it was 9.30 and Koko was still there, waiting for his entrance like the forsaken bride in the music hall song.

'That's it for tonight!' announced a disgruntled Eleanor. 'Perhaps next week we can get a move on. For heaven's sake, look at your scores before you come, chorus, and, as for the principals, learn the libretto before you turn up, otherwise the date of the performance will have to be delayed until much later.'

It was a quiet return to the Vicarage after the rehearsal. I was annoyed that my wife had been so indiscreet in her contretemps with the Curate, and she was equally annoyed that I had intruded into her first attempt at stage direction. Mrs Cooper endeavoured to pour oil on what she could see were troubled waters by asking how the rehearsal had gone. Her kind intention exacerbated the situation. 'Excellent!' I told her.

'How could you be so hypocritical!' snapped Eleanor once our housekeeper had made her way up to bed. So the silence ended in an unholy row in which both participants suffered from voice strain in trying to keep our voices down.

'I'm going to bed,' said my wife.

'Sleep well,' I replied sarcastically. I turned on the television and fell asleep almost instantly. I awoke to an empty screen and a warning noise that the set was still on. When I got into bed Eleanor was sound asleep, to my relief. Seconds later I joined her in oblivion.

Breakfast was as quiet as our return to the Vicarage – apart, that is, from the children, who made up for our reticence with an abundance of decibels. Mrs Cooper decided to take over as major-domo in view of our sullen silence. 'Quiet, children,' she shouted. 'Can't you see that Mummy and Daddy are trying to get some peace? They have got thick heads.'

My wife spluttered into her coffee. 'Quite right, Auntie Cooper,' she managed to say. 'Haven't we, Daddy?'

By now I was trying desperately to control my mirth. 'Yes, Mummy,' I burbled, 'very thick heads.' Once again sanity had been restored to the household by our housekeeper's misuse of the English language, described by Eleanor as a 'God-given gift'.

We parted on amicable terms, I on my way to Matins and my wife bound for the surgery at Brynfelin. Hugh Thomas was in a sober mood and apologized for his irresponsible behaviour at rehearsal. He asked to change his day off to Saturday, when he and his bride-to-be wanted to visit Cardiff to buy kitchen furniture.

I had just returned to the Vicarage when there was a telephone call from Superintendent Brian Williams.

'Well, Mr Rural Dean,' he said. 'We have finished our questioning of the Reverend Herbert John Phillips. I am afraid the man is completely *non compos mentis*. He has been charged with the crime of arson and will appear before the magistrate later this month. From there he will go to the Assizes, where I am sure the judge will order him to be detained at Her Majesty's pleasure, out of harm's way. So, as far as he is concerned, your troubles are over. From what I can see, with your many commitments it is just as well.'

'Thank you, Superintendent,' I replied, 'especially for the speed with which you acted to prevent any further destruction of our churches. I don't know how long we could have kept fire-watching rotas going in the deanery – not very long, I suspect.'

No sooner had I put the phone down than there was another call. My heart sank when I heard the parsonical tones of the Archdeacon, who announced his presence in his usual pompous manner.

'Have you heard anything more about the arrest of the Reverend Herbert John Phillips?' he enquired.

'I have indeed,' I said. 'As a matter of fact I have just put the phone down after receiving a call from Superintendent Brian Williams. It appears that he has been charged with the arson attack on Llanybedw and with the desecration of St David's, Brynfelin. His case will come before the magistrates and then the Assizes, where he will be ordered to be detained at Her Majesty's pleasure, Mr Archdeacon.'

'Oh, good, good,' came his reply. 'Very good indeed, if I may say so. Now then, there is something else I want to speak to you about. When I instructed you to advise the incumbents in your deanery about the need to carefully examine their insurance policies' – his speech was punctuated by split infinitives from time to time – 'I should also have told you that the churches should be locked in between services, main doors and vestry doors locked, securely locked. I know that this is unfortunate for parishioners who might want to come into their church for private prayer, but they can always come to the vicar or rector if they wish to pray privately, and unlock the church for themselves. In other words, the churches must be locked for security reasons but can be unlocked for private prayer, private prayer. Have you got that? Would you like me to repeat it?'

'No, no, Mr Archdeacon,' I replied. 'It is not necessary.'

As I told my wife later, 'I have arrived at the stage in my conversations with his venerableness that I am indulging in triplicate replies.'

'God forbid,' she said. 'Never mind your triplicate reply, what about the extra load of work he has given you? I expect the omission to let you know about the locking of churches in the deanery was a deliberate attack of amnesia.'

'Thank you, doctor, for that diagnosis,' I replied. 'As an amateur I had made the same assumption, based on bitter experience.'

After lunch I decided to pay a visit to Ivor Hodges at the Abergelly Secondary Modern School, to see whether he could duplicate circulars to the deanery clergy about the locking of churches. I had no typewriter. Machines and I were an ill-fitted couple. As far as my car was concerned, I knew how to open and close the bonnet, but what was inside the bonnet was an unknown world. On the few occasions when there was a malfunction, I had to rely on my wife to search for the fault. As for domestic appliances,

I was a complete ignoramus. The replacement of a plug was as much a mystery to me as algebra had been when I was in school. A pen and the telephone were my sole means of communication.

The headmaster was at his desk, wading through a pile of papers. 'It looks as if I have chosen the wrong moment to see you,' I said apologetically.

'Not at all, Vicar,' he replied. 'It's always a pleasure to have your company. Now then, what can I do for you?'

I explained the purpose of my visit. He frowned. 'I am afraid we are not allowed to use school equipment for any other purpose than school business,' he said. 'In any case the Mayor-Elect would be the last person to countenance that.' He paused. 'However, I think I can help in a different way. We have just bought a new duplicator. The old one is a bit ancient but it is still in working condition. You can have it for nothing. It should serve the parish for quite a few years until we can afford to buy a new one. It's about time that we had some office equipment. A second-hand typewriter is the next thing, but I am afraid I can't help you there.'

I looked at him wide-eyed. 'What on earth am I going to do with a typewriter? As you know, I send all the parish magazine matter to the printer hand-written.'

'Well, Vicar and Mr Rural Dean,' he replied, 'it is about time that you moved out of the age of the dinosaurs into the second half of the twentieth century. If you find it impossible to handle a typewriter, then you must find someone who can do it for you. Why not enlist the help of your curate's fiancée? She uses a typewriter in her work. I am sure she will be only too pleased.'

So it was that Janet became my secretarial assistant. Within two days of my conversation with Ivor Hodges, I had procured a typewriter which Dai Elbow had 'wangled', as he put it, from the local office of the National Union of Mineworkers . 'I 'ad a word with Emrys Stephens, the secretary, and 'e told me that they 'ad just streamlined everything and that they were now up to date and didn't need the old-fashioned machines. "So wot the 'ell," he said to me, "if your vicar wants it, 'e can 'ave the old typewriter. Our new one is electrical. It's the only way to fight the Coal Board. Play 'em at their own game. You can't fight tanks with bows 'n' arrows."'

My curate's bride-to-be was only too pleased to offer her services as parochial secretary. By the end of the week, every incumbent in the deanery had been advised of the latest instruction from the Archdeacon.

'Before long,' commented my wife, 'all the parishes in the deanery will be submerged in a deluge of archidiaconal dictates, and I should think that most of them will end up in the wastepaper bin.'

The first hint of this came from the Reverend K.J. Whittle, Rector of Llandeiniol, the north-countryman who had complained that he could not understand the secretary's reading of the minutes at my first Ruridecanal Conference. His parish was a residential district in the outskirts of Newport; the congregation was drawn from the comfortably well-off executives and others of the professional classes who came to the countryside to escape from the hurly-burly of their daily commitments.

'Mr Rural Dean,' he trumpeted in his strong Yorkshire accent, 'I must say that I object strongly to the

Archdeacon's dictatorial instruction that we must lock up our churches. On a point of order, I doubt whether he has the authority to do this. He has not joined the bench of Bishops as yet, and I hope to God that he never gets there. As far as I am concerned, my church will remain open for anyone who wishes to pray in the house of God. If he wishes to dispute my right to do this, I shall take the matter to the Bishop. You can tell him that from me.' With those words he put the phone down. I did not attempt to ring him back.

That phone call was followed by another from the Reverend Doctor Paul Winter, an inoffensive country parson, Vicar of Cwmnafon. He had retreated into the hills of his desolate parish to write a learned thesis on the Pelagian heresy. It had been printed as a paperback which could be seen years later, reposing on church bookshelves, available at a greatly reduced price. He was a mild-mannered man in his late fifties, a bachelor who was bullied by his housekeeper. There were two churches in his parish, both of them medieval and badly in need of repair, but Paul Winter had achieved a lifetime's ambition and was content to wait until retiring age, taking his services and spending the rest of his time in his study. Rarely did he come to a deanery meeting or a Chapter meeting.

'Er, Mr Rural Dean,' he began, 'I, er, hope you will not feel that I am in any way, er, how shall I put it —?' there was a long hiatus as he sought to find a suitable word '— rebellious.' The thought of him as a rebel was hilarious. 'However,' he went on, 'I feel I must protest most strongly at the Archdeacon's demand that we should lock our churches. It, er, only takes one, er, sadly unhinged priest to put all our buildings under this, er, ban. Now that the man is, er, safely in custody, I see no, er, reason why we should follow his instructions. I shall be honest and tell you that I will not, er, conform.'

After three more phone calls of a similar nature, I decided that I would contact the Bishop and ask for his advice. I telephoned the Bishop's palace, only to be informed that he was away for the day but his secretary would leave a message for him.

When Eleanor joined me for our evening meal, she was delighted to hear of the response from the deanery clergy. 'It's about time that the pompous idiot was put in his place,' she said. 'I only hope that his lordship will see to that after he phones you tomorrow. The only comment I shall make is that the Bishop is such a nice man that a rap over the knuckles from him will be more like a gentle touch on the wrist.'

The next morning at ten o'clock, the Bishop phoned me. 'I gather from my secretary that you want some advice. I trust that I shall be able to oblige. What is it, Fred?'

I took a deep breath and began by saying, 'It is about the Archdeacon, my lord. I do not wish you to think that I am making a personal attack upon him. However, over the past weeks he has become a little heavy-handed in his approach to the arson attacks by the Reverend Herbert John Phillips. His latest instruction is that all churches in the deanery must be locked throughout the day. This has brought strong protests from the incumbents. Already I have had five phone calls expressing indignation about the edict. They point out that the arson has been caused by one unhinged person who is now in custody, and that it is the only time that such a thing has happened. They say that people from time to time come into their churches to admire and sometimes to pray. They feel that it is an over-reaction to a one-off event.

'I know that he has said that those who wish to visit the churches can be advised, in the church magazine or by a notice on the door, that a key can be obtained from the vicarage or rectory, but they say that they should not be expected to stay in lest somebody wishes to borrow the key. I am sorry to have to trouble you with this, my lord, but I feel that you should be made aware of the situation.'

It was quite a while before he answered.

'First of all,' he said, 'I can understand the attitude of the Archdeacon. One church, a medieval gem, has been destroyed. Another has been desecrated. So it is inevitable that under the circumstances he is anxious that there will be no repetition. On the other hand, I appreciate the concern of your incumbents who are convinced that there will be no repetition. I shall have a word with him about the situation. He will be here with me next week and together we shall sort everything out, I am sure. Apart from that, is everything else all right?'

'Yes, splendid, my lord,' I replied. 'All is well.'

'Good,' he said and rang off.

No sooner had his lordship ended his call than the instrument announced its presence once again.

'Hello!' I snapped.

'That's not like you!' said Uncle Will of Llanybedw.

'Sorry, Will,' I replied, 'but I have had a surfeit of calls ever since I circulated the clergy about his venerableness's latest orders. I have just put the phone down after a session with the Bishop. I have told him about the disquiet the clergy feel over being told to lock their churches.'

'Well done!' he said. 'Just because poor old Herbert decided to pick on my church to make a bonfire and has now been put out of harm's way, how stupid of that idiot to lock up all the churches. That is why I thought I would ring you.'

'By the way,' I replied, 'the Bishop referred to your church as a medieval gem.'

'And so he should,' he said. 'I'll never get over losing that lovely place.'

We continued with our conversation for some time. Will Evans ended our tête-à-tête with a warning. 'Let me tell you something, Fred. That bugger, if you will excuse the language, will be after your blood for your request for advice from the Bishop, you mark my words.' He was right.

# 5

On the Wednesday morning of the following week, I was closeted in my study struggling with a very difficult *Times* crossword when there came a sharp and persistent ring on the doorbell. I waited for Mrs Cooper to go down the hall with her unhurried tread. The pace of the footsteps quickened after a brief conversation. She tapped on my door and announced that there was a vicar 'with riding breeches' who wanted to see me urgently.

'Shall I show him in, Vicar?' she asked.

'No thank you,' I said, 'I know who it is. I'll go to the door to meet him.'

The dignitary was inside the house by the time I arrived. He was a tall, thin individual with a pasty complexion, except that on this occasion his facial colour was drained into an off-white pallor. Behind his rimless spectacles his eyes had narrowed as he saw me. 'I'd like a word with you,' he managed to utter through his clenched dentures.

'By all means, Mr Archdeacon,' I replied jauntily. 'How nice to see you!'

He followed me into the study, evidently puzzled by my perky attitude in view of his intimidatory display on the doorstep.

'I shan't sit down,' he growled. 'I have to be at the deanery Chapter meeting in Penrilleth at eleven o'clock. Last night I was at a meeting with the Bishop. He informed me that you had complained about the instruction I had given you about the locking of church doors to prevent any further arson in the deanery. You had no right to go to the Bishop about it. Why didn't you object when I spoke to you, or write to me afterwards, or even telephone me later?'

Having completed his trinitarian formula he continued with his tirade. 'What I told you to do was in the best interests of each parish, to protect the incumbent from any further assault upon the buildings in his charge, and to make sure that nothing like the events of the past few weeks ever happens again.'

'This is for the second time of asking,' I said to myself.

'However, I have been told by the Bishop that the churches may be left open provided that all due care is observed by every incumbent, every incumbent, and that every incumbent knows of the change in the arrangements.'

Before I could say anything he had turned on his heels and disappeared from the Vicarage. I went to the study window, only to see the tail end of his aged Bentley sweep up the drive.

Conceding defeat to the *Times* crossword compiler, I removed the newspaper from my desk and wrote a draft of the letter which I would present to Janet for reproduction, informing every incumbent that the mighty had been put down from his seat. I found it difficult to avoid a note of triumph in the circular. It was my first victory over my dictatorial superior. I took pleasure in saying that 'the

Bishop has asked the Archdeacon to rescind the instruction that all the churches in the deanery should be locked'. The only dampener to my elation was the knowledge that I was burdening the bride-to-be with another chore at a time when she was preoccupied with her arrangements for the furnishing of the house and for the wedding ceremony, which was less than a fortnight away.

When Hugh Thomas arrived at St Peter's for Matins next morning, he imparted the information that he and Janet were 'snowed under', as he put it, 'with all the impedimenta of getting married'.

'I am sorry to have to add to your impedimenta, Hugh,' I said, 'but I have an urgent task for your beloved to do for me.'

His face dropped. 'What is that, Vicar?' he enquired.

'The Archdeacon came to see me yesterday,' I replied. 'He was not in a good mood, I may say. In fact, for a man of the cloth, he was positively murderous. The Bishop has asked him to withdraw his dictate that all the churches in the deanery must be locked. So I have to circularize the parishes with the glad tidings.'

He grinned. 'Vicar,' he said, 'that's a task Janet will undertake with the greatest of pleasure. She has only met him once, at her cousin's wedding years ago, when he was Vicar of Llanarfon before he was appointed Archdeacon. According to her, he was like a death's head at the feast. Since then I have told her all about his endeavours to put you down. In the words of Winston Churchill, "give her the tools and she will finish the job".'

Later that evening, the parochial secretary typed the letter and cyclostyled it with the assistance of her fiancé.

When they had finished, I invited them into the sitting room where they joined Eleanor and me in a toast to the Bishop. 'May his successor be as much a man of God as he is,' I proclaimed.

'Why are you talking about a successor when a godly man is still at the helm?' asked my wife.

'According to the birthday list published by *The Times*,' I replied, 'he is 69 today. So my toast was a birthday one, coupled with a pious hope that when he has his next birthday and he has to retire, according to the Constitution, he will be followed by someone worthy to fill his shoes.'

'And not somebody who will put his foot in it,' she added, 'like the reverend gentleman who called earlier this morning!'

'If that did happen,' I said vehemently, 'I should look for a parish in another diocese, much as I should love to see a permanent church on Brynfelin.'

'What about us?' interjected Hugh. 'We should be stranded in a new home without the guiding light who led us there.'

'I have never been compared to the Star of Bethlehem before,' I replied, 'but I feel it in my bones that the Electoral College would not be so deaf to the Holy Spirit that they would appoint him, of all people. There are many other candidates more capable than that man.'

Three days later it was Palm Sunday. Hugh and I had decided that we would bring the children down from Brynfelin to the parish church for the procession of palms at the Family Communion. It was a custom I had inherited from Canon Llewellyn when I was his curate at Pontywen. I should imagine that it was something he had

71

inherited from his younger days. It involved the carrying of bunches of pussy willow with their soft, fluffy buds. On the Saturday, the children would be raiding the river banks and other places to collect their trophies to present in church the following day. I had hired a coach from Edgar Thomas, the Abergelly bus proprietor, 'Continental Tours Our Speciality', and Dai Elbow had volunteered to supervise the boarding of the coach to save the Curate the trouble of making the journey up to Brynfelin. It was a gloriously sunny morning.

Outside St Peter's the first to arrive clutching their ceremonial offerings were the Scouts, who were running amok five minutes later, ignoring the frantic efforts of their Scoutmaster to keep them under control. They were using the branches as weapons in combat with each other. As I emerged from the vestry to find out the reason for the shouting on the church path, William James came up to me in great desperation. 'Vicar, I need your help. Will you please tell the troop to stop their bad behaviour? They are not normally like this.'

Either Willie's memory was blank, or else he was hoping that mine was in a similar condition. Whenever I had been in the presence of his Scouts, they were always badly behaved. I strode across to them and shouted in my best sergeant-major voice, 'Quiet!' They froze into statues at this command, which came from behind the memorial to the Reverend Silas Morgan, the first Vicar of Abergelly.

I went into their midst. 'You are boys who should know better,' I warned them. 'Very soon there will be a crowd of boys and girls, most of them much younger than you. They will be waiting to go into the church in procession. You should be setting an example. Once I have robed

I shall be back out here. If there is any repetition of your outrageous conduct, I shall ask your Scoutmaster to send you home and to notify your parents of the reason for your dismissal.'

I went back to the vestry in complete silence. Five minutes later I came out in my robes to be greeted by Hugh Thomas.

'Sorry I'm late, Vicar,' he said, 'but I have been waiting for our coach to arrive. It has just turned up. There are only twenty-five kids, but about thirty mothers and aunts who took the opportunity of a free ride to Abergelly, and most of the children haven't brought any pussy willow. Dai Elbow has been doing his nut. The women have all disappeared and left their offspring to run riot.'

'It's all right, Hugh,' I told him, 'they will be in good company. Willie James' Scouts are in like condition. It is going to be a lovely service.'

By half past nine, when the bellringers were laying aside their ropes after providing enough sound to drown the chaos outside the porch, the Curate and I, assisted by Tom Beynon and Dai Elbow, were faced with the task of creating an orderly procession to enter the church to the strains of 'All Glory, Laud and Honour'. Despite the reluctance of those children who carried an abundance of pussy willow to share with the have-nots, every child had a branch or perhaps a couple of twigs to hold as they shambled down the aisle to the altar rails. There they were received by me, Hugh Thomas and the three churchwardens of the parish. Dai Elbow revelled in the position of authority, colliding with Tom Beynon and Ivor Hodges as they proceeded to lay the pussy willow on the altar steps.

Twice during the first part of the communion I had to appeal for quiet from the over-excited children. Then came the distribution of the palm crosses for the whole congregation. The presence of the adults in the queue for the sacred emblem of the crucifixion helped to calm the children. However, when I ascended the pulpit for my sermon I was confronted with the sight of the boys in the infant classes, who were in the two front rows, using the sacred emblems as swords in duels with their neighbours. To my dismay, I could see my son as one of the most energetic in this Errol Flynn scenario.

I stood silent for a few minutes as the mayhem died down into a sound vacuum. Then I said quietly, 'I am ashamed, ashamed that some of you are using the symbol of the cross, on which Jesus died, as a sword. What must He think of you?' Faces dropped. 'I hope, when you come up to the altar in a short while, that you will tell Him how sorry you are for what you are doing. When you go home I want you to pin up that cross in your bedroom to remind you that He loved you so much that He died a terrible death to prove it.'

For the rest of the service there was no more misconduct.

It was a false calm. As soon as the children began to leave the church, the boys from Brynfelin began fighting with the boys from Abergelly. This time it was Dai Elbow who intervened. The sight of the big ex-rugby forward moving into the scrum of mauling youngsters, pulling them apart by the scruff of the neck, was sufficient to quell the disturbance. 'Now then,' he shouted, 'those from Brynfelin follow me back to the coach – pronto.' In no time at all they had disappeared.

Hugh Thomas and his bride-to-be came up to me in the porch as I was shaking hands with the few remaining members of the congregation. 'I am sorry about all this, Vicar,' he murmured. 'I shall have some strong words to use at Sunday School next week.'

'Don't worry, Hugh,' I said. 'I shall be equally strong with my words to our lot, including my son and heir.'

'If their mothers and aunties had been in church, this would not have happened,' he went on. 'I am going down to the coach to tell them what has happened and to ask why they were not in church.'

'I should think Dai has done that already,' I replied, 'but it won't do any harm to have you backing up what he has said to them.'

When I returned to the Vicarage, my son was nowhere to be seen. Eleanor said, 'He has gone to ground. He is not in his room. I think he may be hiding somewhere in the garden. Don't worry, he'll turn up when his Sunday dinner is ready. What a dreadful anticlimax it was to all your expectations for a lovely service. Still, it's all over now and I am sure that Palm Sunday next year will be a really enjoyable occasion.'

'I am afraid it is not all over now,' I replied. I was looking out through the study window and I could see Hugh Thomas and Janet coming down the drive in a very agitated fashion. Before they could ring the doorbell, I was there before them. 'Come on in,' I said to them. 'What on earth is the matter?'

'You'll never believe this,' he replied breathlessly. 'The mothers and aunties were told to be back at the coach by eleven o'clock at the latest. It is now nearly twelve o'clock and there is no sign of them. Dai says that it's murder on the coach, with the boys fighting each other instead of the Abergelly kids.'

'I have more than a shrewd suspicion that the "aunties" are not relatives, but drinking partners,' I said. 'They are probably down on the riverside sunbathing and imbibing.'

'So that's why they were carrying shopping bags when they got off the coach,' replied my disconsolate curate. 'I thought they were carrying pussy willow inside.'

'Sorry, Hugh,' I said. 'It was the fruit of the hops, not the willow. If you go down to the banks of the River Gelli, I am sure you will find the missing passengers.'

He and Janet left the Vicarage in the highest of dudgeon. My curate's fiancée found herself yards behind her beloved as he strode up the drive to pick up his car from outside his digs.

'So much for our outreach on the Brynfelin estate,' I remarked to my wife.

'Well, you can't make a silk purse out of a sow's ear,' she replied. 'Let's face it, Fred, you are dealing with people who have come from the backstreets of the town, most of them feckless, apart from the few who are like Janet's parents, responsible and only too glad to have their own home instead of living in rooms. Believe me, I know these families who come to my surgery, preying on the National Health.'

'You amaze me,' I said. 'You are the woman who chose to minister to these benighted folk instead of setting up a practice in town. You felt sorry for the way in which they had been dumped in a God-forsaken wilderness by the town council.'

'Don't get on your high horse,' she retorted. 'The fact that they did not get the facilities provided for them, which an enlightened local government should have given them, does not detract from the fact that they are the kind of people who cannot fend for themselves. Of course I am sorry for them, and I care for them in my own specialized way. That does not mean that I think they can all be replicas of Janet's parents. They will never be like that in a month of Sundays, believe me.

'My dear love, your task is a much greater one than mine. I care for their bodies. You have to care for their souls, and may God help you in that, because no one else can.'

It was at this stage in our conversation that there was a timid tap on the study door, as if the tapper was fearful that it would be heard. 'Come in, David,' I said, in my best Mr Squeers voice. There was a fumbled attempt to open the door. I went to assist in the opening.

A tearful countenance confronted me. 'I didn't want to upset Jesus. Honest I didn't.'

His mother went past me and swooped him up in her arms. 'Of course you didn't darling, did you? It's the last thing you would ever do, isn't it? There you are, Dad, he is very sorry, so I am sure you will forgive him, won't you?'

After those three questions, ending in a direct one to me, I had no option but to pardon my errant son for his transgression. I kissed his head as he lay in his mother's embrace. 'I am sure you didn't mean it, David,' I said quietly. 'You didn't realize what you were doing, and I am positive that He knows that.'

He looked up at me. 'Thank you, Dad. If you tell me that He knows that, I am sure that He will forgive me.'

Suddenly a little voice came from the open doorway. 'David'th a naughty boy, ithn't he?' This was one question too many.

'Elspeth,' demanded her mother, 'get back up to your room and don't come down until dinner is ready.'

When Hugh Thomas came to Matins next day, he was still seething with indignation at the way in which the mothers and 'aunties' had behaved.

'I drove down to the recreation ground,' he said, 'only to find the women stretched out alongside empty beer bottles and singing "Roll Me Over in the Clover".'

'What song is that?' I enquired.

'It's rather obscene, Vicar,' he replied, 'and certainly not suited to Palm Sunday. When I informed them that the coach had been waiting for them for over an hour, they were abusive rather than apologetic. I told them that they were unfit to be mothers and that this was the last time that I would arrange transport from Brynfelin to Abergelly for a church service. Dai Elbow was furious when they arrived, and addressed them in terms which were suitable for the occasion. Like me, he told them that this was the one and only time that they would have a free outing to Abergelly. By the time the coach left it was in an atmosphere more like a funeral than a celebration of Palm Sunday. When I got back to my digs for my last Sunday dinner in Abergelly, I began to wish that it was my first.'

'Come on, Hugh,' I said. 'Let's say our prayers and listen to what the Bible has got to say to us. I am sure that the Old Testament prophets and the New Testament apostles had to face much more daunting tasks than ours in this parish.' With his shoulders bent and a frown on his face, he preceded me into the chancel.

The first lesson came from the book of Lamentations, ending with the words, 'Is it nothing to you, all ye that pass by? Behold and see if there be any sorrow like unto my sorrow.' He read this with heartfelt passion. This was followed by the Te Deum with its ascription of praise concluding, 'O Lord in thee have I trusted, let me never be confounded.' This was followed by the opening verses of St John in the fourteenth chapter: 'Let not your heart be troubled; ye believe in God, believe also in me.' As I read the prayer for Palm Sunday in which we were exhorted to 'follow the example of His patience', I wondered how Hugh would react to this beautiful collect. Once in the vestry, after the service, I asked him if the service had helped to lift the gloom which had settled up on him.

'To some extent,' he replied. 'I was encouraged by the Johannine message not to be troubled, but much more so in the collect where we were urged to "follow the example of His patience". Patience has never been my strong point. I suppose this is the penalty of youth. You want to conquer the whole world in a moment of time. Anyway, I must learn to "knuckle down", as my form master used to tell me in school. It is only now that I realize the size of the challenge that Brynfelin presents. All I can say is that I shall do my best. At least I shall have a home of my own and a lovely wife with whom to share it.'

As Holy Week progressed, the thoughts of the parish were focused more on Easter Monday than Easter Day. My curate had shown himself to be a much-loved priest who was a caring man of God, not so much on the Brynfelin estate, where his ministrations were largely unknown in the impersonal world of the indifferent, but in the confines of Abergelly, where he had established himself as someone whose charismatic personality had made him a host of friends.

Not only that, but his forthcoming marriage to a local girl added interest to the event. The decorations to the parish church for Easter Day took on an added perspective. His forthcoming matrimony was not only featured in the gossip columns of the local newspaper, but also in the sporting coverage of the back pages, where his promise as an outside half was described as a 'sacrifice of a Welsh cap' by his devotion to this beloved.

Janet and her mother spent most of the week cleaning the house and putting up curtains, in addition to laying down the carpets which had been ordered from Cardiff. When Hugh invited me to inspect their home on Easter Eve, it had all the hallmarks of a comfortably furnished residence, unlike the working-class interiors of his neighbours' houses. This was due to the generosity of his middle-class parents, who had spared no money in providing their one and only son with the comfort to which they thought he was due. I wondered how long it would be before resentment would set in among the more deprived on the estate that such an affluent young man could be given a council house.

On Easter Day there was a record number of communicants at the parish church. It was the custom that all the offerings on that day were given to the incumbent to be counted by him at the Vicarage. Tom Beynon suggested at

Evensong, where once again there was an unprecedented large congregation, that I would be up all night counting the collection. 'Mind, Vicar,' he said, 'as they do say in the Bible, the labourer is worthy of his hire, so enjoy the fruits of your labour.'

When Eleanor and I sat down at the dining room table later and began to open the envelopes, it was soon apparent that the labourer had been handsomely rewarded for his toil. The total was the magnificent sum of one hundred and eighty pounds, seven shillings and ninepence, the equivalent of a third of my yearly stipend. Many of the envelopes contained notes, mainly of the ten shilling variety.

'Well, my dear,' said my wife, 'this shows how much they appreciate your ministry.'

'Perhaps I should put half into the church building fund,' I suggested.

'Don't you do anything of the sort, Frederick,' came the vehement reply. 'Your congregation have given that to you as a gift for your own personal use. You can use a modicum of it by taking me out for a celebratory dinner later this week. Why not spend the rest on a replacement for your ancient Ford?'

'Another example of the empathy between us,' I said. 'I have just been thinking of using the money to get another car.'

'That is not empathy,' she replied, 'it is called common sense!'

The next morning I arose from my slumbers and opened the curtains to look out on a very wet morning. 'Last night's weather forecast was right for a change, love,' I said. 'It is piddling down!'

'What an unclerical expression!' said Eleanor. 'It's a good thing that Miss Edwina Lewis did not hear it. As a vicar's daughter and leader of the Girl Guides in this parish, she would have been shocked, to say the least. However, more important, love, is how disappointing it is for Hugh and Janet. Perhaps it will clear by twelve o'clock.'

'By the look of the sky, that will be a miracle,' I replied.

'Well, it is a clerical wedding,' she said archly. 'So you never know.'

As the morning wore on, it was quite evident that a miracle was not about to happen. The clouds which had settled on the hills around Abergelly looked like permanent fixtures. I went into the church hall after breakfast, where preparations were in full flow for the wedding reception. Hugh's parents had wanted a function in the Cambrian Hotel, the town's only hostelry with a three star entry in the RAC guide book. However, their son had insisted that the event should be more of a parochial occasion, something the ladies of the congregation had welcomed with eager anticipation.

As I came through the door I was met with the happy chattering noise fitting to a nuptial event. Tom Beynon was carrying a large trestle table, with Dai Elbow in vociferous support at the other end. ''Ere we are, ladies!' he was shouting as a group of approved members of the Mothers' Union awaited its arrival in front of the stage, where it was designated to be the top table. Around the hall, volunteer waitresses were laying tablecloths on the smaller tables which had already been erected. Vases of flowers lay on the floor, ready to be placed in position when the time was ripe for their decorative purpose.

In the kitchen, a large ham was being sliced by Les Jones, the local butcher, watched by an admiring audience of the churchwardens' wives, who had been given priority in the food preparation. 'The secret, ladies, is to be delicate in your approach. You don't attack it, you just gently caress it with this sharp knife.' Not for nothing was Les known as 'Les the ladies'.

As I left the hall, Janet's parents were arriving to see how the preparations for their daughter's marriage were progressing. 'She's at the hairdresser's at the moment,' said her mother. 'I'm afraid the poor girl is in a state of panic. Perhaps having to sit down quietly while her hair is being attended to will help to calm her down. We are just popping in to see that everything is going smoothly, and then after that we shall be back home before she gets in.'

The rain was beginning to ease by the time I had reached the Vicarage, but the clouds were still covering the hilltops.

At half past eleven I made my way to the church. By now there was only a drizzle. The Scouts and the Guides were to form a guard of honour, since both the bride and the groom had been members of the organizations in their youth. It was only recently that the Guide company had been formed by Miss Edwina Lewis, who had come to live in Abergelly after the death of her father, the Vicar of Treafon. She had been living at the vicarage and had bought a house near the parish church. As school teacher and an ardent Guider, she had asked me if she could form a Guide company in Abergelly. I was only too pleased to oblige, since it would help keep the little Scoutmaster in his place. It was unfortunate that Miss Lewis had been away over the Palm Sunday weekend, otherwise the presence of the Guides might have quietened the riotous behaviour of the Scouts.

Miss Lewis had arrived already and was in earnest conversation in the porch with two of the ushers, who were armed with the printed leaflets containing the hymns and the psalm for the service. She was diminutive in stature but, unlike Willie James, she was large in circumference. Dressed in her uniform, which fought to contain her sheer bulk, she looked as if she might explode through the hard-pressed buttons at any moment. Her rosy-cheeked countenance, the product of a healthy outdoor life when released from the classroom, was focused upon the young gentlemen prop forwards of the Abergelly rugby team. They looked at me as if I was a referee who had blown his whistle to save them from an awkward predicament at the base of the scrum.

'Hello, Vicar!' they chorused.

'Not a nice day for a wedding,' added Llew Philips, sixteen stone and, like Miss Lewis, bulging out of his suit.

Before I could reply, the Guide captain chided him for his remark. 'Young man, the wedding is more important than the weather. First things first.' I made my escape to the vestry, leaving the 'young man' wide-eyed at the reproof.

As I was opening the safe to get the registers, Dai Elbow appeared, resplendent in a newly bought outfit, double-breasted, check-patterned, which only required a bowler hat to make him a walk-on comedian. A large red rose adorned his buttonhole. ''Ome-made, that,' he informed me. 'I'm not partial to carnations. Now then, is there anything I can do to 'elp, Vicar?'

'You can indeed, Dai,' I said. 'You can light the candles on the altar to save me a job. After that you can put the hymn numbers up on the board, to save one of the choir-boys running loose in the chancel. The hymn list is here on the desk. That will be fine, thank you.'

A quarter of an hour passed in which I was able to fill in the marriage details undisturbed. I could hear the noise from the nave as the excited guests were taking their places, and also an equal number of decibels from behind the closed door of the choir vestry. Then it opened with an accompanying order for 'silence' from the organist and choirmaster. Graham Webb came up to me with the news that all the choir were present, with not a single absentee.

'Where is the bridegroom?' he enquired. 'There's less than ten minutes before the service is due to start.' I looked at my watch. 'I'm off to the organ,' he said. 'Give him my best wishes and tell him that I am expecting to hear his tenor come through in the hymns.'

When the opening voluntary thundered into life a few minutes later, the bridegroom and his best man were still not in evidence. I went out into the chancel to see if they were in the front pew. The church was crowded, but that seat was empty. Back in the vestry I put on my robes and once again examined my watch. There was one minute to go.

Suddenly I heard footsteps approaching up the chancel. Hugh and his best man, college friend and confidant, the Reverend David Parry, loomed into the doorway.

'He's lost his voice,' said David.

# 6

I have never seen anyone as desperate as Hugh Thomas on his wedding day. He threw his hands in the air as soon as he saw me. I was about to ask him when it was that he had been struck dumb, only to bite my lip as I realized that I would add to his frustration if I did so.

'The bride will be here any minute now,' I said, 'so we had better decide on a plan of action. Before the service begins, I think I must tell the congregation that you have lost your voice and that you will mouth the words.'

No sooner had I said this than Dai Elbow erupted into the vestry with the news that the bride had arrived. 'Go and tell the choir to process into the chancel!' I instructed him. 'You and David go down to the front pew,' I said to the inarticulate bridegroom. 'That will end any speculation about the reason for the empty seat.'

Once the choir had moved into the chancel I made my way to the porch, amid the subdued conversation of the large congregation. When I reached the open door, I found a very nervous bride on the arm of an equally nervous father. In her bridal array, the olive green two-piece costume bought from the most prestigious store in Cardiff, she looked the epitome of Celtic virginity with her dark hair and brown eyes. Her two bridesmaid friends from the chorus of the Gilbert and Sullivan Society, in their rose pink dresses provided a vivid contrast with their beaming, excited smiles.

'Come on, Janet, my love,' I said. 'This is not a dentist's appointment, it's your wedding. So cheer up!'

She attempted a brief indication of happiness by showing her teeth for an instant. Her father was unable to relax his facial muscles.

'By the way,' I added, 'Hugh has lost his voice.'

Janet's eyes opened wide and her mouth dropped. 'How will he be able to make his vows?' she asked, as tears began to well up.

'Don't worry, love,' I assured her. 'I have told him to mouth the words. That will be sufficient. I once had to marry a deaf and dumb couple. At least your voice is intact.' So saying, I signalled to the organist to begin the Wedding March. Everybody stood and we began to make our way down the aisle.

We reached the chancel steps where a worried bridegroom was standing, accompanied by his best man who looked as if he had not a care in the world. As Hugh turned to see Janet, his frown disappeared, to be replaced by a smile of loving admiration. This was reciprocated by the bride, who had to be reminded that she must transfer her bouquet to her senior attendant.

'Now, before we begin this service,' I announced, 'I have to inform you that the bridegroom has lost his voice.' This was greeted by a mixture of giggles and sounds of solicitude. 'So when there is no audible reply to my questions and no declaration of a plighted troth, will you please accept the fact that Hugh has not turned his back on his delightful bride, but has indicated to his very best ability that he has wholeheartedly made his vows in the presence of God and this congregation.'

It was the most impressive marriage service I have ever conducted. There was total silence during the exchange of vows, which was only broken by the heartfelt contribution from the bride. When they came into the vestry at the conclusion of the service, there was such a warm embrace between the betrothed that it was only broken by the arrival of the minor players in the sacrament of Holy Matrimony. By the time that kisses and handshakes had been exchanged, it must have been at least ten minutes before the bride and groom were ready to process through the full church to begin their married life.

Inside the church porch they ran into chaos as the Guide Captain and the Scoutmaster were in contention as to which side of the church path should be occupied by their respective charges. As the rain beat down in torrents outside and the noisy participants in the guard of honour were engaged in verbal exchanges, I decided to intervene in the interests of law and order.

'Quiet!' I bellowed, with such ferocity that I frightened myself in the process. I coughed after the injury to my throat. 'Will the Guides and Scouts please go back into the church,' I croaked. 'It is far too wet to stand outside in this deluge.'

I turned to Hugh and Janet, who were engaged in conversation with the disconsolate photographer, Mansel Williams of the Abergelly Academy. Mansel could see a lucrative event in the process of being destroyed by the weather. 'Might I suggest that a few photographs of groups framed by the arch of the porch and a plethora of others taken in the church hall will fill the bill?' I said. 'Two seconds outside in that rain would produce images of drowned rats, if you will pardon the expression.'

'Excuse me, Vicar?' enquired Mansel. 'What did you mean by that word about the photographs in the church hall?'

'All I meant was that you can take as many as you like indoors,' I replied.

'I know that,' he snapped, 'but they won't be the same quality by flashlight. That's what worries me.'

Hugh tapped him on the shoulder and gave him the thumbs up sign. 'You do the best you can, Mr Williams,' interpreted Janet. 'I'm sure everything will be fine.'

So, scorning the protection of the umbrella, the intrepid photographer took a number of shots of the couple, the bridesmaids and the immediate family, before retreating with them to the church hall. Then followed an undignified exodus of the congregation, some with umbrellas and the others with improvised means of shelter, varying from the service leaflets to up-raised crossed arms.

As I made my way to the vestry to disrobe, I was confronted with the spectacle of the Scouts and Guides indulging in a race down the side aisles.

'This is not a sports stadium,' I shouted. 'Will you please all sit down until you are ready to go home, Guides on one side and Scouts on the other.'

Inside the vestry, Graham Webb was divesting himself of his surplice. 'When I get back to school next term,' he said, 'I am going to have a word with that lot out there, both the boys and the girls. I would have thought that Miss Lewis would have had more control over her charges, with her reputation for discipline. Evidently she is all bark but no bite.'

'My dear Graham,' I replied, 'Miss Lewis was not aware of what was happening, unlike Willie James, who has no control over his charges. She was engaged in the porch in a long conversation with two old ladies who chose to stay there until the rain abated. Her entry into the nave coincided with my strong words to the relay racers. I think you would be wise to confine your words to the boys.'

I opened the door to check on the weather. To my relief I found that the watery stair-rods had been replaced by a gentle drizzle. 'Thank God for that!' I exclaimed.

When Graham and I emerged into the chancel, the Guide Captain was ablaze with indignation as she lectured her girls. 'I don't think they will give a repeat performance,' whispered the organist. On the other side of the aisle, Willie James was addressing his troop, who were giggling and apparently deaf to his words, since all their heads were directed towards the females on the other side of the aisle.

I waited until the Guide Captain had finished her tirade. 'You will be pleased to know that the rain has eased off and you will be able to go home,' I announced.

'Girls!' ordered Miss Lewis, 'you stay here until the Scouts have made their way out. I know it is supposed to be ladies first and then gentlemen next, but since there are no gentlemen opposite, stay where you are.'

With that, there was an explosion of activity as the non-gentlemen scrambled their way out of the pews in a mad dash to be first out of the church, leaving behind a traumatized Scoutmaster who could only gawp at the exodus.

'Now then, Guides,' commanded their Captain, 'will you stand and go up the aisle in twos, in an orderly fashion.' It was a dignified procession, rendered all the more impressive in comparison with the unruly behaviour of their male counterparts. Willie James looked as if he would have been more than grateful to have been swallowed up and never seen again.

We entered the church hall to join a queue of guests waiting to be received by the principal participants in the ceremony. Members of the female chorus of the Gilbert and Sullivan Society were on hand with trays of sherry to greet those who had run the gauntlet of introduction. Hugh's voice was showing signs of incipient audibility, perhaps produced by one of the ushers surreptitiously supplying the means of lubrication. Janet's father and mother were wilting under the strain of the many handshakes, while Mr and Mrs Thomas were revelling in the occasion. The bride had found a hitherto undiscovered source of self-confidence because of her partner's unforeseen silence.

Pinned to a blackboard placed at the side of the entrance of the hall was an elaborate plan of seating, provided care of the council office where Janet was a valued employee. Once the guests had taken their glass of sherry, they queued up once again to find their places at table. In the meanwhile, the voluntary waitresses in their Sunday-best outfits plus aprons were making last-minute checks on the plates of hors d'oeuvres which were positioned ready for the attention of the diners.

No sooner had the last guest been along the reception line than Mansel the Snaps indicated that there were a few more groups he would like to include in the album of memorabilia, especially since the Vicar had been absent when he had taken the photographs in the church hall. I was aware of the impatience of both guests and helpers to begin the meal. To this end I suggested to the photographer that he should make the exercise as brief as possible. Wiping some rain-sodden locks from his brow, he assured me that it would be all over in two ticks.

According to my wristwatch it was ten minutes per tick. By the time we were all seated for the meal, the wedding breakfast had become more like afternoon tea.

I joined Eleanor at the top table, where she was showing signs of exhaustion as she listened to Janet's grandmother. 'Another thing, doctor,' she was saying, as I moved into the chair at the side of my wife, 'I get these palpitations sometimes when I lie down to go to sleep.'

Before she could get a free medical opinion, there was a loud tap on the table by the best man, who invited me to say grace. This was followed by much scraping of chairs on the freshly polished floor as the assembly rose to its feet. I waited for complete silence before I said the simple grace which preceded our meals at the Vicarage. 'Bless O Lord, these gifts to our use and ourselves to Thy service.' One day I hoped I would have courage to say what the church organist had intoned when called upon unexpectedly to say grace: 'O Lord, open Thou our lips, and our mouths shall show forth Thy praise.'

By the time everybody had resumed their seats, the old lady had forgotten what must have been the umpteenth item on the bulletin of her ill health. Eleanor heaved a sigh of relief as she turned to me and said, 'This is Janet's grandmother. She has just told me that she is 82. She looks the picture of health, doesn't she?'

'Pleased to meet you, Vicar,' she whistled through her ill-fitting false teeth. 'I've heard a lot about you from Janet. She's a good girl and she'll make Hugh a good wife. I said when she was only a little girl, she'll make somebody a good wife one day. Mind, I never thought she would be a parson's wife. We've never been big churchgoers. I was brought up Baptist but I turned Congregational when I married Albert. Not that we went often 'cause he used to work Sundays a lot in the steelworks.'

Welcome relief came with the tureen of hot potatoes and other vegetables to accompany the delicately carved cold ham I had seen provided as an entertainment by the local butcher for the delight of the churchwardens' wives. For the next quarter of an hour there was a merciful release from the verbal onslaught, as the grandmother's teeth clicked their way through a full plate without leaving a morsel. The same omnivorous process disposed of a large dish of home-made trifle before Eleanor and I had reached the halfway stage. As soon as she had finished her eating she resumed her talking.

'Well, as I was saying, doctor, I get these palpitations sometimes when I lie down. I can't go to sleep because it's like having a drum beating away. Do you think I should put some cotton wool in my ears?'

My wife had her mouth full and was unable to answer. She was occupied in caressing my leg with her foot under the table. Eventually, once she had swallowed her portion of the sweet, she replied, 'I am afraid, Mrs Rees, cotton wool is not the answer. The only cure for that, as I told you about your indigestion, is not to eat anything in the evening. Would you excuse me, please? I have to dash back to the Vicarage to see if my two children are happy with their babysitter.'

I wondered what Mrs Cooper would say if she heard herself described as a babysitter. It was quite obvious to me that Eleanor was at the end of her tether. Furthermore, I doubted whether she had gone to the Vicarage. I decided to seek her out in the kitchen.

'Perhaps I had better join my wife, Mrs Rees,' I said, thanking God that I did not have to lie to make my escape as the old lady turned her attention to the bridegroom's aunt. I vacated my chair with an enormous sense of relief.

In the kitchen I found my wife sipping a glass of white wine and looking pleased with herself.

'Were our two children happy with the babysitter?' I enquired. 'You realize that you will never go to heaven,' I went on. 'A parson's wife telling fibs to a dear old lady!'

'Now *you* are telling fibs, Frederick,' she riposted. 'A dear old lady! She was a self-centred hypochondriac who had spent an eternity criticizing her family before you appeared on the scene.'

'Well, she did say that Janet was a good girl,' I replied.

'That's because you are the Vicar,' said Eleanor. 'She thought she would make the right impression by doing that, and evidently it paid off. I suggest that we stay out of the way until they cut the wedding cake by going up on the stage before the Mothers' Union arrives on the scene with the dirty dishes.'

'Are you inviting me to some hanky panky behind the curtains?' I whispered.

'For heaven's sake, Frederick,' she hissed. 'Grow up. I may have given you some tootsie footsie under the table while the "dear old lady" was present. That was simply to preserve my sanity in the face of octogenarian persecution by reminding myself that my husband was at hand.'

No sooner had we made our way to a row of chairs than quite suddenly the curtains were opened, revealing a card table covered by a lace cloth on which the wedding cake reposed. I had forgotten that Hugh had asked that the cake be cut on the stage, where he and his bride had spent so many happy hours over the past year. Now there was not only a cake to be seen by the audience, but the Vicar and his wife with a glass of wine in her hand. There followed a round of applause, obviously not directed at the cake.

'Before the postprandial round of toasts to the happy couple and the bridesmaids begins,' announced Eleanor, 'my husband and I would like to propose a toast to the Gilbert and Sullivan Society, which has brought Hugh and Janet together, as the Major-General and one of his daughters, on this very stage. I trust they will not proliferate their progeny to the extent of that gallant soldier's production. Please stay seated as I say, "Here's to the Abergelly Gilbert and Sullivan Society, and long may it prosper."'

Then she raised her glass and emptied it in a flash. As I gazed at her in unbounded admiration, her impromptu escape from embarrassment was greeted by her listeners with great enthusiasm. She turned to me and whispered in my ear, 'Follow that, Secombe.'

'I couldn't in a month of Sundays,' I replied. 'If I had a hat on I'd take it off to you. I tell you what, I was petrified. There's only one thing: what are we going to say to the dear old soul?'

'Nothing,' came the laconic answer. 'By the time we resume our seats they will be cutting the cake, then will come the toasts. Perhaps once she has had a couple of glasses of wine she will be too fuddled to remember where I was supposed to have gone.'

So it was. The rest of the proceedings were received in silence by the grandmother, who returned to her tête-à-tête with the bridegroom's aunt after the last speech.

The most interesting of the speeches was the one by the bride, who read out what had been scribbled by her husband on the back of the order of service and a couple of paper doilies. In it, apart from a few stumbles over badly written words, Janet's delivery was impeccable. Her voice was clear and pleasantly pitched. To my amazement, when she had finished her script she put it down and addressed the guests directly.

'That was my husband,' she said. 'Now this is me. I doubt if I will ever again have the chance to be our spokesperson. I am more familiar with the typewriter than with anything else. All I can say is this. I am very proud to be Hugh's wife. I love him very much. I hope I will be worthy of the love that he has for me. Thank you.'

She sat down to a prolonged ovation, blushing, with her eyes downcast, only to be embraced by Hugh, who was obviously moved by her sincerity and her deep regard for him.

As Hugh's father remarked later, the brief speeches by the two ladies were by far the best contributions to what Eleanor described as the postprandial efforts of the males.

There was bright sunshine to welcome the departure of the couple on their honeymoon. My curate had taken great care that his ancient sports car was roadworthy for their journey to Port Isaac in Cornwall. Janet's olive green two-piece suit provided an attractive contrast to her husband's college blazer with its gold stripes on a sable background. Evidently Hugh had decided that it was better to spend money on his honeymoon than on a new suit. 'In any case,' said my wife, 'they will need all the cash they can get to complete the furnishing of their little grey home on the hill.'

The car roared away, in typical Hugh fashion, and the well-wishers outside the church hall dispersed after kisses and handshakes, with promises to keep in touch that would be forgotten as the months rolled by. It was a scene I had witnessed many times in my ministry.

We went back into the kitchen where the Mothers' Union were busy washing up and gossiping, while in the hall Tom Beynon was supervising the dismantling of the trestle tables. Dai Elbow was telling him what a sacrifice the Curate had made by giving up his rugby for the sake of his beloved.

'Apart from 'is side step and 'is distribution of the ball, 'is kicking was the best of any outside 'alf Abergelly 'ad ever 'ad. It was 'is trajectory that was perfect. I've never seen a trajectory like it, not even at Cardiff Arms Park. A wonderful trajectory.'

It was evident that Dai was in love with the word, which he had taken pains to pronounce correctly. He must have seen it written in the *South Wales Echo* in a report of a match, or perhaps heard it spoken in the sports programme on the wireless. Wherever he had found it, he had clung to it in a warm embrace. He had used it to me several times in relation to Hugh. I wondered what answer he would give if I asked him what it meant.

Ten minutes later I went into the kitchen, where Eleanor was helping with the drying of the last of the church hall crockery. As she laid down her towel, she said, 'Well, Vicar, shall we go home now?'

'With pleasure,' I replied. 'We shall be able to find out if our two children have been happy with their babysitter.'

'Where is Mrs Cooper, then?' enquired Katie Webster.

'With the two children,' said my wife. 'It's just the Vicar having his little joke. He has probably had too much wine.'

The following evening was the annual Easter Vestry meeting, when churchwardens were appointed, church accounts presented, and a new Parochial Church Council elected. This was followed by the Vicar's appraisal of the previous year's progress, or otherwise, in the life of the parish. Like the municipal elections, this annual event did not engender much interest among the congregation, so at the last Parochial Church Council Ivor Hodges, my warden, had proposed that we should bribe the electorate with some kind of reception involving tea and sandwiches, which would precede the meeting. A suggestion from Dai Elbow that alcohol should be included had been turned down. As Tom Beynon said, 'This is a time for clear heads, not a Christmas party atmosphere.' The reception was due to begin at seven o'clock, to be followed by the business agenda at 7.30, the sacred time for all church meetings.

When I went into the church hall at a quarter to seven, I arrived simultaneously with Miss Lewis, Guide Captain and an aspirant for a seat on the PCC. She was carrying a plate of sandwiches. 'I thought I would make a contribution to the refreshments,' she informed me. 'I know I have not long been in the parish but I would really like to be a part of it. I was a member of my father's PCC for years up until his death.'

I remembered her father well, a large, bulky man whose daughter had inherited his weight but not his height. He was a chain-smoker whose fingers were permanently stained by the tobacco. On the only occasion I was invited into his study, I was amazed to see its walls covered by stacks of newspapers. Apart from his large desk and a small bookshelf, there was little else but the product of Fleet Street. It is small wonder that his sermons were said to be based on the *Daily Telegraph* rather than the Bible.

As we went into the kitchen, she said, 'Oh, by the way, Vicar, I must apologize for the behaviour of the Guides on Saturday, when they took advantage of my absence to run riot, incited by those dreadful Scouts. I can assure you that there will never be a repeat performance. I intend to keep a tight ship, believe me. I have always had discipline in my form at school and discipline in the Guide companies I have had under my control.'

She was greeted by the few lady members of the PCC who had formed themselves into a small catering committee for the evening. Edna Evans, a supervisor at the local clothing factory and a long-standing member, suggested that she thought it was time she stood down in favour of Miss Lewis. She said she would propose the Guide Captain. The vicar's daughter glowed with pleasure. I left the scene with an uneasy feeling that trouble might lie ahead in the not too distant future.

In the hall the churchwardens and some of the male members of the PCC were putting out chairs, anticipating a bigger attendance than usual for the evening. Sid Thomas, the portly little secretary, was thumbing through the minutes of the last meeting behind the large table which had served as the focus for countless annual vestry gatherings.

'Well, it's a nice dry night after all the rain we've been having,' said Tom Beynon, 'so nobody can blame the weather for a poor turnout.' He need not have worried. Soon there was a large influx of the congregation, including several who had never been present at this important occasion.

When Eleanor arrived she came up to me and expressed her amazement. 'Frederick!' she exclaimed, 'What a crowd! Isn't it unbelievable what a cup of tea and a few sandwiches can do? I think Ivor Hodges deserves a hearty vote of thanks at the next PCC meeting for his brilliant wheeze.'

The cup of tea and a few sandwiches took longer to consume than expected, and it was not until almost eight o'clock that the meeting got under way. In the meanwhile, much bonhomie was engendered, unlike my first vestry meeting in Abergelly which had been an ill-tempered affair. After the minutes, read at breakneck speed by Sid Thomas, had been approved, I proceeded to give my annual 'state of the parish' address. I was pleased to report a considerable increase in the number of communicants and in the number of the newly confirmed. Church finance had received a considerable boost by the Midnight Matinée, which featured my brother, but the amount of money needed for the erection of a permanent church on Brynfelin was still a daunting figure.

When the balance sheet for the year was presented by the church treasurer, Alan Roberts, an accounts clerk in the council office, Miss Lewis raised the question of the Easter offerings omission from the circulated copy she had been perusing. He explained that it had always been the custom in the parish to give the offertories to the vicar directly, since it was the congregation's gift to him and as such should not be recorded in the church register.

'I must say,' replied the lady, 'it is most unusual to let the amount go unrecorded. My father was always presented with a cheque at the Easter Vestry.'

Tom Beynon was on his feet. 'We are more than happy in this parish to make it a private matter for our vicar. What happens in other parishes is their concern.' His remarks were received with grunted approbation. 'I move we accept the accounts with thanks to the treasurer for his work.' This was carried unanimously after it had been seconded by Ivor Hodges.

Then followed the elections. Tom Beynon was re-elected, I appointed Ivor Hodges as my warden once again, Dai Elbow was elected warden at St David's. After the Guide Captain's query about the Easter offering, I wondered if she would be elected to the Parochial Church Council. One by one the present members were proposed and seconded.

'I propose Mrs Edna Evans,' said Alice Greenway. I waited to see if she would announce that she was not standing this year. Nothing was said. 'I second that,' said Tom Beynon. Miss Lewis' face was a deep scarlet. Eventually the list was closed without the inclusion of that lady.

There were three new members on the PCC. I welcomed them heartily and thanked the three deposed for their diligence over the past year. I said that I looked forward to working with all the elected officers over the next twelve months, and closed the meeting with the grace. Miss Lewis made a rapid foray into the kitchen to collect her plate and left the hall looking as if she would have had great pleasure in hurling the piece of china at Edna Evans.

As Eleanor and I relaxed in the Vicarage with our nightcaps, she said, 'What a good thing our Guide Captain was not elected to the PCC. She would have been a perpetual thorn in your flesh.'

'You don't know how near a thing it was,' I replied, and told her what had transpired in the kitchen before the meeting.

'Thank God for Edna Evans and her *volte face*,' she exclaimed. Then she added, 'Mind, if she had been proposed, there would have been no one to second her. I don't think she will ever be a popular member of the congregation. Perhaps she will transfer her allegiance elsewhere.'

'No such luck,' I said. 'She will be just as unpopular wherever she goes. At least as long as she remains in this parish, she still has the Guides over whom she can assert her authority.'

# 7

'I have just had a very interesting conversation with Robert Williams,' said Eleanor when she came home for lunch. It was some three weeks since Hugh and Janet had returned from their honeymoon in Cornwall. Robert Williams was a family doctor with a surgery in the main street in Abergelly. He and my wife had been fellow students years ago. Robert was Janet's doctor from childhood. Although Eleanor's surgery was only a few streets away from her home, the Curate's wife thought it inadvisable to have the Vicar's wife as her physician. 'Well, perhaps "disturbing" is a more accurate adjective than "interesting",' she went on. 'Janet is pregnant.'

'A honeymoon child,' I suggested.

'Very much a pre-honeymoon pregnancy,' she replied. 'The poor girl is at least three months into her pregnancy. He has told me this in the strictest confidence.'

'I should think so,' I said. 'Where is his Hippocratic oath? I always thought that everything told to a doctor never went outside the surgery.'

'Look here, Secombe!' she snapped. 'I always thought that anything told to a priest was equally sacrosanct. How many times have you told me what has been said to you, presumably in confidence? Robert passed on this information because he knew that tongues would wag when her condition became evident. That time is quite near. You will have to wait until Hugh tells you. At least you have been forewarned. Under the circumstances it is a pity he did not apply for that curacy some months ago.'

'All we can do,' I replied, 'is to hope that the congregation will turn a blind eye on the calendar. As you know, he is very popular. It would be a pity if we had to lose such a good priest.'

I did not have to wait long for Hugh's confession. It came the very next day. He arrived in the vestry for Matins, white-faced and obviously very nervous.

'Before we go into church for Matins,' he said, 'do you mind if I get something off my chest? I have been meaning to do it over the past few weeks and haven't had the courage to tell you.' He took a deep breath. 'Janet is pregnant. In fact she was pregnant when you married us. I don't know whether this affects my position in the parish, or in the diocese, if it comes to that.' He raised his eyes from the floor and looked me full in the face. It was a look which was a mixture of anguish and pleading.

'First of all, Hugh,' I replied, 'when is the baby due?' He seemed to be taken aback by my reply. 'The doctor says that it will be in six months' time.'

'No wonder you lost your voice at your wedding,' I said. 'Do your parents know?' He shook his head. 'I should think your father will be very surprised when you pass on the news. As a doctor he will think that his son has been very remiss in his sexual relationship with his partner. If he could not contain himself until his marriage, at least he should have known the need for contraception. You have been very foolish, Hugh.

'As far as I am concerned, I do not wish to lose you. I shall not report you to the Bishop. There is one snag. If the Archdeacon gets to hear of your premarital indiscretion, he will certainly report it to the Bishop and also report me for not informing his lordship. We shall wait and see.

'There is one other thing. Once the congregation become aware of Janet's condition, tongues will wag. Let's hope that the pregnancy will not manifest itself too early and that people will think it is a honeymoon child.'

By now his face had changed completely. His colour had come back and the tension had gone from his face. He shook my hand warmly. 'I thought you would have given me my cards,' he said.

'Don't think you are out of the woods, Hugh,' I told him. 'Indiscretions like yours have a nasty habit of causing trouble when you least expect it. All that is required is for some malicious person to write to the Bishop – or, worse still, to the Archdeacon, who would be only too pleased to exploit the situation. On reflection, I think it would be better if I contacted the Bishop. He is most understanding. Then if the Archdeacon does get hold of the news, he can do nothing about it. The Bishop will have been informed already. Do you mind if I do that?'

There was a pause while he thought about it. 'You're quite right, Vicar,' he said quietly. 'News is bound to come out, sooner or later. I would much rather the Bishop knew than the Archdeacon.'

Eleanor was about to leave for her surgery when I came in from Matins. I told her that Hugh had informed me about Janet's pregnancy. 'What did I say when Hugh was pushing you into getting a house for him?' she remarked. 'I told you it sounded suspicious but "no," you replied, and bit my head off for suggesting a pregnancy.'

'Well, my dear,' I said, 'a few months ago you suggested that Superintendent Brian Williams might be an arsonist. Anyway, I have told him that I shall inform the Bishop immediately before our Archdeacon gets hold of the story.'

'Wise move, Frederick,' she replied, then she kissed me and made a hurried exit to her car, which was standing in the drive with its engine running. She always liked a quick getaway.

Later that morning I phoned the Bishop. 'Good morning, Fred,' he said genially. 'What can I do for you?'

'I should like to see you about my curate. It is a private matter which I would not like to discuss with you over the phone. It is not urgent but I would like to see you in the not too distant future.'

There was a pause at the other end of the line and a turning over of leaves in the episcopal diary. 'As they say,' replied the Bishop, 'there is no time like the present. If you can be with me by 2.30 this afternoon you can have your discussion.'

'Thank you, my lord. It is very kind of you.' I put the phone down with a sigh of relief. The sooner the matter was over the better for all concerned, I told myself.

At half past two I was met at the door by the Bishop. 'Come in, Fred,' he greeted me. 'You are looking very well, I must say. You must have caught last week's sun.' I was ushered into his study and sat down in a comfortable armchair facing his desk. 'Now then, what is the matter for discussion?'

I leaned back, savouring the comfort of the chair, and began the speech I had been preparing on my way to the episcopal residence. 'Some five weeks ago, as you know, Hugh Thomas was married in the parish church. Now he tells me that his bride was pregnant at the time of the marriage. He is deeply conscious of the deception involved in what I thought was the union of two people who had a premarital relationship of non-sexual indulgence. Hugh is a very fine parish priest with a love of his people, a gift of preaching and an acceptance of the challenge of an estate built by a council with more regard for the houses than for those who live in them. It would be a tragedy if he had to walk out of a situation where his priestly gifts are solely needed. That in a nutshell, my lord, is my contribution to the discussion.'

The Bishop looked at the notepaper on his desk and stared at it for some time. Then he raised his head and with his eyes half closed, delivered his considered judgement on the situation vis-à-vis my beleaguered curate.

'There is no doubt at all that Hugh Thomas has set a bad example to his flock by his lapse in sexual conduct. How can his congregation look up to a man who has no control of his sexual appetites? On the other hand, he is not a philanderer but has given up his career as a sportsman for the sake of his relationship with the girl who is now his wife. From what you tell me, he is devoted to his calling and is an excellent parish priest. I could suggest that he moves to another parish, or even to another diocese. However, taking into account his undoubted qualities in his ministry and, from what you have told me in the past, the high regard in which he is held by his people, I would suggest that he remains in his patch in the parish. Such a benighted population needs love from its pastor. I am sure that they will forgive the lapse on his part. Undoubtedly there will be eyebrows raised when it becomes apparent that there is a big discrepancy between the time of the birth of the baby and the marriage of the couple, but "let him that is without sin cast the first stone".

'So, my dear Fred, I would suggest that you do nothing to exacerbate the plight in which this young man finds himself. I shall write to him expressing my displeasure at his misconduct and inviting him to come and see me some time next week. I shall then deliver a stern warning to him about his future behaviour and leave it at that.' He stood up and announced that he had to go to a meeting of the Diocesan Committee for Moral Welfare at 3.30. We shook hands warmly and I made my way to the new Ford I had bought, courtesy of my Easter offerings.

As I drove home, I began to sing, 'Praise God from Whom all blessings flow and from our dear Bishop here below'. When I had driven from Abergelly to the cathedral precincts I had had no idea that my mission would be so fruitful. I knew his lordship was a man of God. I could not wait to get back to the parish and to let Hugh Thomas know that the Lord had looked kindly upon him. From now on, it was up to him to repay the Almighty for His goodness towards him. Knowing my curate, I was convinced that he would do this in full measure.

It was a lovely spring afternoon, blessed with sunshine. As I came from the verdant pastures of the countryside into the grime of the industrial valleys, even Abergelly's terraced houses took on a different aspect. Since my curate would be out visiting on the estate, I decided I would call on Tom Beynon, that master of discretion, who was on the six till two shift, and let him know in confidence of Hugh Thomas' indiscretion. It was half past three, by which time he would have been fed by his wife and watered by the local brewery, and was possibly sitting back in his chair in the middle room, spreading his foul fumes of cheap pipe tobacco to the annoyance of his long-suffering partner.

I knocked long and hard at the door, without any response. As I stood outside, the next-door neighbour emerged, looking concerned. 'I'm afraid, Vicar, that Tom has been taken to hospital. He was injured in a fall at the colliery this morning. I don't think it is anything too serious, just a broken leg and a couple of ribs, according to Margaret. She has gone to visit him. She told me she had tried to ring you but you had gone to see the Bishop.'

In a matter of minutes I was at the reception desk in the hospital. Before I could enquire in which ward he had been placed, the receptionist informed me that it was the Evan Davies Ward. 'I've known Mr Beynon since I was a child when we lived next door to him. He was more like an uncle than a neighbour. I don't think he has been badly injured, a broken leg and some ribs broken as well – but that's all. He'll be glad to see you, Vicar. Tell him that Nerys George sends her love. I'll tell you what, Vicar, he'll be out of that bed in no time, knowing him.'

As I entered the ward, I was greeted by a loud shout. 'Vicar! I'm down here in the corner.' There was my warden with his plastered leg suspended in the air, his face unscathed and his vocal powers undiminished. His little wife, seated beside him, was admonishing him. 'Tom, keep your voice down. The Vicar can see where you are without you bawling at him. He's got eyes in his head.'

On my way down to his bed, I passed several invalids who would have been glad of his rude health, most of them enjoying the remainder of the afternoon's siesta – those, that is, whose deep sleep had not been disturbed by my churchwarden's fortissimo summons.

I pulled up a spare chair on the other side of his bed. 'Nerys George sends her love,' I told him. 'She was on duty at the reception desk when I came in.'

'Lovely girl,' said Tom. 'I watched her grow up.'

'So she said,' I replied. 'Now then, what has happened to bring you in here?'

'I'll go and get a cup of tea while you get the saga,' interjected Mrs Beynon. 'That will take at least a quarter of an hour.'

'Women!' exclaimed Tom, as she made her way out of the ward. 'Well now, in answer to your question, at about eleven o'clock this morning, I was down at the coal face, singing away – 'Guide Me O', I think it was – when all of a sudden there was a crack. The next minute I was buried underneath some best anthracite. Evan Rees, who was working a few yards away, came down and pulled away the coal from me. "Don't worry," I told him, "I feel fine." That was until I tried to sit up and then I felt this pain in my leg and in my ribs. He got in touch with the surface and in no time at all I was up at the top with an ambulance waiting for me.

'It looks as if I won't be any use to you for a couple of months. But there, it could have been that I would have been permanently out of this world. Evidently the Almighty thinks He's got some more I can do for you in St Peter's.'

I decided that this was not the time for me to inform him of the Curate's predicament.

'My dear Tom,' I said, 'it is quite obvious that the Lord has kept you on earth for a purpose. Many years ago, Eleanor and I were on holiday on the North Wales coast. A brother and sister who were staying at the same hotel offered me their canoe for a paddle up and down the low water. Unfortunately, I have no gumption. Instead of steering the craft parallel to the shore, I found myself heading out to sea. Fortunately there was a rocky promontory, with the tip of which the canoe collided, overturning the craft and depositing me into the depths of Cardigan Bay. As I cannot swim, I told myself that if I came up, my only hope was to cling to the canoe. Just as the Almighty preserved you, so He did me. As I bobbed up to the surface, I clung to the canoe like grim death. I was towed in ignominiously by the brother and sister, to the great relief of Eleanor, whose laughter at my upending quickly turned to alarm when she remembered that I could not swim.

'Tom, you and I have been spared to carry on the Lord's work. Let's hope we shall be worthy of the opportunity.'

'Well, there's a story,' commented Tom. 'As you say, it looks as if the Almighty has got a job for us to do. I hope you don't think it – what is the word? – er, flippant, if I tell you another story about the seaside. Dai and Tom, two miners, were on a day trip by train to Aberystwyth. They got in a carriage where there was a commercial traveller sitting on his own. He started telling them stories about what he was supposed to have done. Then he said, "What about you? You must have a story to tell."

'Dai said to Tom, "You tell him that story about Aberystwyth."

' "A couple of year ago we was going up there, just like we're doing now. It was a lovely 'ot day, so we decided to go for a swim. We're very good swimmers. Well, we didn't 'ave no costumes, so we went to the end of the beach and went into the water with nothing on. We'd been swimming about 'alf a mile out when suddenly I saw a shark come up behind Dai. Just as it was going to grab 'im with its big jaws, I pulled out my penknife and stabbed it in the back. The sea was full of blood and we swam back as fast as we could."

' "Amazing," said the commercial traveller. "But wait a minute – you said you were naked."

' "Yes," said Tom.

' "In that case, where did you keep that penknife?"

' "Oh, I can see," said Tom, "it's not a story you want. It's a bloody argument."

'I hope you will excuse the "bloody", Vicar, but it takes away the effect if you don't say it.'

'Quite right, Tom,' I replied. 'From a hospital invalid it was a very funny story, especially since it's only a matter of hours since you were attacked by a load of best anthracite, as you put it. I think I had better leave you now and come to see you tomorrow, especially as your dear wife is returning.'

He winced with pain as he moved to shake my hand. 'You don't have to come and see me tomorrow, Vicar,' he said through gritted teeth. 'You've got enough on your plate as it is.'

'I am not promising to stay long,' I replied, 'but I am sure I can spare ten minutes or so for my right-hand man.'

He smiled as Margaret took her seat beside him. 'Hear that, love, the Vicar has just said I'm his right-hand man.'

She patted his hand. 'And I'm your right-hand woman, aren't I – a fat lot of good you'd be without me looking after you.' She planted a resounding kiss on his cheek, to my warden's obvious pleasure.

When my wife came in later I told her of the accident and Tom's breezy reaction to it.

'I'm not surprised at his insouciance, if I may demonstrate my O-level French,' she said. 'He has been pumped full of drugs to counteract the trauma he has suffered. When you see him in the morning, you will find an entirely different Tom Beynon, after a night in which he will suffer extreme discomfort, to say the least. Now then, my dear, what was the outcome of your visit to his lordship? Are we to lose our invaluable curate or not?'

'That is the good news,' I replied. 'If ever there was a man of God our diocesan is surely that. He said that Hugh is obviously a good priest and the very man for the job in Brynfelin, so the Curate can continue in the parish. He will wish to see him in a week or so's time to warn him that his future conduct must be that of a man of God and an example to those in whose charge he has been appointed. I was going to see him immediately on my return, but Tom's accident has put an end to that. However, once we have had our evening meal, I shall pass on the glad tidings before he leaves for the youth club.'

'Excellent,' she said, 'but he will need to be prepared for some behind-the-hand whispering as Janet's pregnancy develops in the next few months. Calendars will be read in Abergelly as avidly as the *Evening Echo*.'

Janet answered the door to me when I rang the bell. Their house was one of the few in the street which boasted an alternative to the knocker. It was the first time I had seen her since the wedding. Already there were signs that her figure was beginning to lose its slimness. Her suntan had faded but was replaced by a blush which enhanced her appearance.

'To quote my first vicar, who had come out of the Ark, is the master at home?' I asked. A glimmer of a smile brightened her countenance.

'He is indeed,' she replied, 'and he will be very pleased to see you.' She paused. 'I hope.'

At this stage in our doorstep conversation, my curate appeared behind her. 'In answer to your greeting my dear Janet, he will. May I come in?'

'In that case,' she said, 'with the greatest of pleasure.'

I was ushered into the new armchair from David Morgan's Cardiff store and sat facing two expectant faces. 'Well, Hugh, the Bishop says that he is prepared to allow you to continue with your ministry on Brynfelin. He will be asking you to go and see him in a week or so's time, when he will warn you to behave in a manner becoming to your vocation as a priest. I have no doubt that you will live up to such a standard. You are not a libertine but someone whose love for your partner was too strong to repress. Anyway, here you are, my dears, it is the green light to serve your people on the hill for as long as you like, and I trust that it will be for quite a while to come.'

Janet came across to me and embraced me. 'Vicar,' she said, 'you are a love.' This was not the shy young lady who tried to hide herself when the Earl of Duffryn visited St David's, or the timorous bride who appeared in the porch just some weeks ago. Evidently the Curate's loss of voice at his wedding had given his wife self-assurance, a gift from the Almighty which, as long as the couple remained in the parish, never left her.

Hugh shook my hand. 'All I can say is that I shall never forget your kindness. I was fully prepared to be cast out into the wilderness.' He put his arm around Janet. 'Believe me, Vicar, I promise you that the labourer in this part of the Lord's vineyard will be worthy of his hire.'

'Very biblical, Hugh Thomas,' I replied, 'and, if I may say so, greatly to be praised. Now then, to return to more earthly matters, the people's warden at St Peter's is in hospital with a broken leg and damaged ribs after an accident at the Point Sarn Colliery. He is in remarkably good spirits. My wife tells me that that is due to the drugs he has been taking.'

'I should think Tom would be better off with a bottle of stout,' said my curate. 'Anyway, I hope it is not a serious fracture. St Peter's will not be the same until he returns.'

'As far as I can gather, I expect he will be on duty on crutches in a few weeks' time,' I replied. 'That is, if the orthopaedic specialist will allow it. In any case, my wife will have something to say to him should he overstep the mark.

'Just one more thing before I go. Please don't think that everything is going to be plain sailing. There are always those who will be only too ready to point the finger at anyone who is in the public eye. Since you were biblical in what you quoted to me, Hugh, earlier on, these are the Pharisees and they abound not only in those who are churchgoing, but in those who never come near a church. You must be strong, knowing that your bishop, your vicar and the bulk of your congregation are giving you their full support.'

'Not to mention my wife,' he said, and kissed her. I left them with their arms around each other as they stood in the doorway.

A few days later it was Dai Elbow who alerted me to the unwelcome news that rumours were already beginning to circulate about Janet's pregnancy. I had told him and Tom Beynon about the Curate's predicament. It was Saturday morning and I was busy preparing my sermons for the following day. As yet I had not informed Ivor Hodges, but I had phoned him that I would like to see him that afternoon. I was engrossed in Bishop Gore's commentary of St John chapter eight, verses 13 to 15, when there was a ring at the doorbell. Mrs Cooper had taken the children out with her to do some shopping while Eleanor was engaged at her Saturday morning surgery.

I was surprised to see the St David's churchwarden on the doorstep. He was accustomed to spend that time of the day exercising his greyhound for the evening stint at the races. 'Can I have a few words with you, Vicar?' he enquired, his brow crinkled by anxiety.

'By all means, Dai,' I replied. 'I am doing my sermon, but I can certainly have a few words, as you say.'

He sat on the edge of his chair, obviously concerned at the tidings he was bringing.

'Well, it is like this,' he began. 'Our next-door neighbour, who is a bit of a hypeecondriact, was at the doctor's yesterday when she saw Janet going into the room where the midwife do do 'er examinations or wotever they do. She said that she looked a bit fatter than she ought to be, like. She asked my missus this morning if she knew anything. Of course, she said she didn't know nothing, but that old biddy is a real gossip and before long everybody in the street will 'ave 'eard. I thought I'd better come and let you know. It will be a pity if poor old Hugh's got to put up with a lot of stick already. When the baby is born, it will be the talk of Abergelly. Mind, 'alf of those who will be opening their mouths will 'ave 'ad their man using their wedding tackle long before they ought to 'ave done. I like that boy and the last thing I want is for 'im to 'ave 'is name dragged through the mud as if 'e was rubbish.'

'Thank you, Dai,' I said. 'I was hoping that nothing would come out into the open for a few months yet, but I suppose that was too much to expect. I suppose in one way, it could be a good thing. By the time the baby is born it will be old hat and everybody will be saying how lovely it is and so on. We'll see. In the meanwhile, we shall have to play it cool.'

That was not how Ivor Hodges saw it when I called on him that afternoon. First of all he showed ill-concealed annoyance that he had had to be told about the Curate's indiscretion by Tom Beynon when he visited him in hospital on the previous day, rather than having the information provided by his vicar. Then he felt that it would have been wiser to have given Hugh Thomas notice on the grounds that his position as a priest would be permanently flawed in Abergelly.

'I know that both you and the Bishop are soft-hearted and well-intentioned. However, that young man and his wife will never live down the consequences of their thoughtlessness in this parish. It will be like an albatross around their necks, and it will not be nice for their child to be brought up in such circumstances. A move to a parish in another diocese would have been the answer to their problem.'

When I took communion to Tom Beynon after the church service the next day, I told him what his fellow warden had said. 'Nonsense!' he exclaimed. 'All that Hugh has got to do is to brave it out. That will be a lot better than running away. I know the people of this parish much more intimately than Ivor Hodges. I was born and bred here. He came from Newport to be headmaster in the town. I tell you what, they will think much more of Hugh if he stands his ground, and I'm sure that is what he will do.'

On Monday morning I had a phone call from the Archdeacon. 'I have had a letter today from a Mrs Perkins, widow of a former churchwarden of Abergelly, Amos Perkins. Mrs Perkins informs me that your curate, Hugh Thomas, was married a few weeks ago in the parish church. According to her, the bride was pregnant at the time. She says that this will cause a scandal in the parish. I am afraid that I shall have to let the Bishop know now before it becomes more widely cognizant. I take it that you knew nothing of this?'

'Thank you for ringing, Mr Archdeacon,' I said. 'First of all, Mrs Perkins has not worshipped in this parish since the resignation of her husband, who was a troublemaker. Second, I do not know where she obtained this titbit of gossip. Third, yes, it is true that Mrs Thomas was pregnant at the time of their marriage. Fourth, my curate let me know about it on their return from their honeymoon. Fifth, I have been to see the Bishop and he has decided to admonish the young man and to allow him to continue his ministry in Abergelly. This is because he is a fine parish priest whose work on Brynfelin is of paramount importance. That, I think, takes precedence over prurient interest on the part of those who do not attend church in Abergelly.'

There was a silence at the other end of the phone. It seemed an age before the dignitary managed to murmur just three words. 'Thank you, Vicar.'

# 8

'What an exciting life you lead,' remarked my wife as she brushed some stray hairs from the jacket of her best suit. 'A week or so ago you had to contend with the consequences of your curate's excess of passion with his beloved. A chat with his lordship at his episcopal palace is followed by a most satisfying put-down of your bête noire, his trinitarian venerableness, and now an honoured seat in the Council Chamber at the mayor-making of Alderman William Stewart. Boy, are you hitting the big times!'

We had decided that I should divest myself of my cassock once the formal proceedings were over in the Chamber. I had no desire to parade in clerical garb in the festivities which would follow the installation. Eleanor was wearing the smart two-piece suit which had caused comment at my curate's wedding since it was almost a replica of his bride's costume, the only difference being in the shade of green. As she said afterwards, 'It just proves that we both have good taste.'

There was a ring at the door. It was Edwards the Taxi, 'We Aim to Please. Distance No Object'. My wife had decided that we should ride to the town hall in a hired vehicle since we would be engaged in a considerable amount of imbibing, knowing the Mayor-to-be's love of the bottle.

'There's quite a crowd there already,' Charlie Edwards informed us. 'Alderman Stewart is very popular, especially since he revealed all that corruption that was going on with some of the councillors. Mind, I expect that gang will have it in for him if he puts a foot wrong, I can tell you.'

When we arrived at our destination I kissed Eleanor and made my way to the Mayor's Parlour, carrying the suitcase which contained my cassock and the newly purchased white bands which were to decorate the garment. As I approached the opened door of the sanctum, my ears were assaulted by a volume of noise more appropriate to a rugby match than a mayor-making ceremony. To quote W.C. Fields, I carved my way through a wall of human flesh to reach Alderman William Stewart. His high-pitched voice had acquired a multiplicity of decibels due to excitement and the whisky glass he was emptying rapidly.

'Ah! Vicar!' he exclaimed. 'Or should I say Chaplain? Put that case down and come and meet some of my friends and my family.' I was introduced to so many in the throng in such a short space of time that my head was reeling. 'First,' he shouted to the overworked council employee who was in charge of drinks, 'some whisky for the Chaplain, Dai.' Dai produced a tumbler and filled it with whisky after refilling the tumbler in the hand of his new boss. I wondered how much distilled spirit he would have to dispense during the next twelve months, particularly into the glass of the chief citizen of Abergelly.

Some ten minutes later a gowned official came to the door and announced that all relatives and friends should take their seats in the Council Chamber. There was some hasty swallowing of the complimentary liquids, followed by a scrum in the doorway. I left my half-emptied glass on a table decorated with fresh flowers and took up my case to enter the small changing room. In doing so, I collided with the tall figure of Councillor Llew Bartholomew, the retiring Mayor. 'Here we go,' he said. 'Dressing up for the last time.'

'Are you sad about it?' I enquired.

'To tell the truth, Vicar,' he replied, 'I'm glad it's all over. In twelve months your life isn't your own. It was all right for the first few months, but as time goes on you wish you were back at work with the boys at the steel-works, and home with your missus. Well, it's William's turn now. I expect he will enjoy it more than me. He is retired, so it will give him something to do.' We emerged from the cubbyhole, he resplendent in his robes, his chain and his cocked hat and I in my new cassock and bands, clutching my book of prayers for all occasions. I wondered how the mayoral gown would look on the short, dumpy figure of the new dignitary compared with the long, lean frame of his predecessor. I remembered what had happened when I had assumed the clerical robes of an incumbent with whom I had exchanged parishes for a cheap holiday. Halfway down the aisle to celebrate my first mass, I caused mayhem in the dignified procession by tripping over the alb and falling flat on my face. I am five foot seven and he was six foot two. I could foresee trouble ahead.

There were now only four of us left in the parlour. The fourth member of the quartet was the Town Clerk, Peter

Williams, a burly embodiment of officialdom who oozed self-confidence.

'Now then, Alderman,' he said to the Mayor-Elect. 'Shall we run over the procedure once more. At the announcement of our entry, everyone will stand. The present Mayor will precede you, followed by the Chaplain. I will bring up the rear. As you know, you will go to the chair on the right of the centre once the Mayor has taken his place and you, Chaplain, will occupy the chair on the left. Then everyone will resume their seats. At this stage in the proceedings I shall read out the charge. This will be followed by the transfer of the regalia to you. After that, the Chaplain will say prayers and the ceremony will be over. You will then make a short speech appropriate to the occasion, in the course of which you will indicate the identity of your deputy. That's about it. Now shall we go?'

As we moved down the corridor which led to the Council Chamber, the Town Clerk tapped me on the shoulder. 'Don't forget,' he said, 'the chair on the left.' He and the Archdeacon were evidently like 'two lovely berries moulded on a single stem', to quote the Bard.

The hubbub within the political powerhouse of Abergelly was stilled by the loud announcement of the usher. 'Will you all stand, please?' The procession to the civic throne was punctuated by the Mayor-Elect's frequent stops to greet his acquaintances, which resulted in the sitting incumbent occupying his seat some time before he was joined by his successor. An irate Town Clerk was breathing fire behind me, doing an archidiaconal repeat of 'What does he think he is doing?' When we were in place, in the accredited positions of authority, Peter Williams spat out his charge. Then followed the transfer of the regalia. It was not so much a transfer as an all-in wrestling match, applauded with relish by an amused audience. I waited for the result before leading the assembly in prayer. The squat figure of the new Mayor was enveloped in the red robe which completely obscured the mayoral chain, while the cocked hat was tilted at a raffish angle.

'Bless the people of this borough,' I prayed, 'and guide with Thy heavenly wisdom our new Mayor, William Stewart, that he may ever keep before his eyes the vision of that heavenly city whose foundations are laid by its Maker and Builder, Jesus Christ our Lord.'

'With his hat over one eye and his sight impaired by his devotion to the spirit,' commented Eleanor after the ceremony, 'he would have had great difficulty in keeping any city before his eyes, let alone a heavenly one.'

After the prayers the new Mayor rose to deliver his inaugural address. By now his hat had been set in a more becoming position on his large head and the robes parted to reveal the mayoral chain in all its glory. 'Well, here we are,' he began. 'I've waited for this aus – er – auspicious occasion for many years, from the time when I was first elected as councillor for the, er, Penderry Ward. I was only – er, what was I then? Let me see …' We waited while he counted up to the correct number of years. 'Thirty-nine, that's it, and here we are.' It was evident that the chief citizen was in danger of incoherence. 'Well, as I said,' he continued, 'here we are, at last, shall I say? Now where do we go, er, from here?'

By this time the Town Clerk was sitting on the edge of his seat, ready to answer the question posed by the Mayor. 'Back to the Mayor's Parlour.'

Suddenly Alderman William Stewart recovered his equilibrium, undoubtedly after many years of practice. 'I intend to see this borough become the pride of the valley, a pearl of great price. Let us see our schools lead the way in, er, scholastic circles, our streets be cleaned of fish and chip papers and so on, our council houses be as good as those who've got mortgages.' Peter Williams buried his head in his hands, knowing full well that the Mayor had no authority whatsoever to wave such a magic wand. After ten minutes more of Utopian promises, he finished his peroration with a plea for full support in his campaign. This was met with lukewarm applause from his fellow councillors and enthusiastic clapping from his family and friends. His reign had begun.

During the buffet lunch which followed in the hall of the civic building, a basement approached by a series of stone steps, much was eaten and even more was drunk. It was fiesta time in Abergelly, financed by the ratepayers of the borough. The queues for food and drink became increasingly disordered as time went by. Good manners were at a discount as guests and councillors fought at the municipal troughs.

'I forecast a plethora of stomach disorders and alcoholic headaches in the community tomorrow morning,' commented my wife. 'I should think that it will affect the attendance at your civic service.'

'Not at all,' I replied. 'Don't forget that this is an annual exercise for which the council has been well trained.'

'I am not thinking of the councillors,' said my wife. 'Like Sir Joseph Porter in *HMS Pinafore*, William Stewart has a large retinue of cousins, sisters and aunts and other relatives, not to mention the male side who are very prominent in the rush for free beer.'

'Since we are in the G and S world,' I replied, 'may I remind you of Pooh-Bah's reference to family pride. Whatever their physical condition, I am sure that the Stewart contingent will drag themselves to church come what may.'

When we left the hall the Mayor was still standing, albeit with eyes glazed. 'See you in the morning,' he managed to say. It was amazing that he could remember that he had to attend church on the morrow.

At breakfast next day, David and Elspeth were discussing the service to be held later that morning. My daughter, airing her five-year-old knowledge, enquired why the important man coming to the church should have the same name as a 'she-horse'. David, three years her senior, was equally keen to demonstrate his command of the English language.

'That's because it's got different spelling,' he replied scornfully. 'When you're older, like me, you'll know the difference.'

'Right you are, clever clogs,' I said, 'you spell the words so that Elspeth will know the difference.' He stared at me, his face strained by the challenge I had given him. 'The word for a – er – female horse,' he said triumphantly, 'is m-a-r-e.'

'Correct,' I told him. 'Now then, the word for the most important man in town.'

There was a long pause during which his brow was knitted and his bottom lip disappeared as prey to his upper teeth. 'M,' he said emphatically, 'er, y (pause), er ...'

'Ten out of ten,' I announced, 'for spelling the female horse, and nought out of ten for spelling the title of the gentleman who is coming here later on. He is the m-a-y-o-r, so don't be such a show-off, David. When your sister is as old as you are, then I am sure that she will be able to spell that word correctly.'

This provoked the pout which was my son's silent mark of displeasure. 'Don't pull a face like that on a Sunday,' said his mother. 'If it is still there when it is time for church, you had better stay here with Auntie Cooper. I'm sure God would be insulted if you came into His house looking like that.'

David decided to beat a retreat to his room to give himself sufficient solitude to compose his features. He loved all the big occasions in St David's, especially if they involved something out of the ordinary. Dressing up in his Cub uniform was the latest fascination for him. To be excluded from the church parade would be devastating.

Marion Morgan, the deserted wife of Gareth, the former churchwarden of St David's, Brynfelin, had offered her services as Akela. In the space of five weeks, she had a pack of some sixteen Cubs which outnumbered the fourteen Scouts in Willie James' troop, much to his chagrin. She found great consolation in the company of the little boys, who were compensating for the loss of the family she had hoped to begin before her husband left her. Already David was her most devoted admirer. Akela was the next best person in his life, apart from his parents. School teachers were not in the same category.

There had been some friction between Hugh Thomas and me about the appointment of Marion as leader of the pack in St Peter's when it should have been in Brynfelin, where it was essential that anything which would involve the children of the parish should take precedence. I pointed out to him that, first of all, Marion had wanted to come down to the town away from the scene which had caused her so much distress, and, second, that there was already an established troop into which the Cubs would proceed when they were old enough. He was forced to acknowledge that my argument was valid, especially since, if Marion were told that she must begin in Brynfelin, she would refuse to co-operate. 'Beggars can't be choosers,' he murmured in response.

After the fiasco of the Curate's wedding, when the Scouts and Guides had clashed and provided an unwholesome spectacle, I was determined that there would be no guard of honour for the Mayor and the council. However, I arranged that behind the pews allotted for the dignitaries, the uniformed youth of the parish would be in their places before the municipal entourage of Abergelly arrived. As the bells of St Peter's began to ring out at half past ten, I made my way to the church with my son, his face transformed into a picture of happiness. He had spent some minutes inspecting himself in the hall mirror. 'Even Solomon in all his glory was not arrayed like one of these,' said my wife to me when she discovered his posing. 'Isn't it amazing what a uniform can do to promote self-importance, or is it self-confidence?'

Outside the porch Marion Morgan was engaged in earnest conversation with Edwina Lewis, vicar's daughter, the formidable Guide Captain. It would appear from the snatch I heard that Miss Lewis was questioning the younger woman on why she had chosen to work with little boys instead of little girls. 'If I had a family, I would pray that they would all turn out to be boys.' She looked around to see me standing with David. 'Like this one, for example,' she added and gave him a hug.

The Guide Captain turned away from Akela to greet one of her Guides. 'Laura, you look a proper mess. Your hat is all over the place and why aren't you wearing your badges? It's not every day that the Mayor comes to our church.' Marion looked at me with eyebrows raised.

I left David in the care of his beloved Akela and went into the vestry, where Graham Webb was in a foul mood because his choristers had promised to be present at half past ten for a rehearsal of the anthem, and only two had appeared so far. 'It's not as if they were *au fait* with the music,' he snapped. 'The tenors were groping for the notes on Friday. God knows what they will be like today. I bet they will not be here until five to eleven.'

'I think I had better go down to the porch to welcome the members of the council and the Mayor's relations and friends,' I said. 'Perhaps you will find they will arrive in a rush.' He snorted.

Outside the church the congregation was beginning to assemble. Inside, Dai Elbow was in charge in the absence of Tom Beynon, who must have been fretting in his hospital bed. Dai had at his command a phalanx of six sidesmen, with hymn books and prayer books at the ready. Against the background of the pealing bells, the chatter of those who had attended the mayor-making was not as excited as it had been on the previous day. Pale faces and shadowed eyes testified to the large input of alcohol involved in the inauguration of the Mayor. The only arrival at the porch unscathed by the jamboree was the central figure himself, fresh-faced and fortified by the hair of the dog as he breathed a jovial reply to my greeting.

'What a lovely morning, Chaplain,' he squeaked. 'What a lovely do yesterday. Just the right start to a year in office.' Since I doubted whether he could remember what he had said in his address, perhaps it was just as well that he thought it was 'a lovely do'. I escorted him and his Mayoress, plus his deputy Mayor and Mayoress and the Town Clerk, to the front pew. Graham at the organ was pulling out all the stops in one of Elgar's 'Pomp and Circumstance' marches as we made our way down the aisle.

Once I had ushered the mayoral party into their places, I went into the vestry, where there was turmoil. My curate was assuring the three tenors that he would help them in the anthem. Apparently they had been cut to the quick by Graham's invective when they arrived too late to rehearse. The girls, who had turned up on time, were also annoyed, because their choirmaster had refused to practice Purcell's 'Rejoice in the Lord Always' without the presence of the men. The four basses had come into church at the same time as the tenors, but had escaped his wrath because they were note perfect.

As Llew Jones, aged 70, said to me, 'I've sung this anthem so many times before, I don't need the book. Why he wanted us here for another go at it first before the service, I don't know. The tenors weren't all that bad. I've heard worse.'

Damned by faint praise, Malcolm Lewis, a 20-year-old recruit, retorted, 'If I had been in the choir as long as you,

Llew, I could have sung it in my sleep and with a better voice than that.'

'Gentlemen, ladies,' I announced in a loud voice. 'We are about to enter God's house to sing His praises, to say our prayers and to listen to His holy word. Shall we have a moment of silence before I say the vestry prayer?' Then, led by 16-year-old Trevor Matthews, server and non-chorister, carrying the processional cross, we made our way into the chancel to the loud accompaniment of the remains of the 'Pomp and Circumstance' arrangement by the organist, who seemed to be venting his spleen on his instrument.

The hymns were sung with fervour while the choir led the rendering of the two psalms impeccably. Hugh Thomas and Ivor Hodges read the lessons impressively. However, when it came to the anthem after the third collect, it was obvious that there was more than a small degree of uncertainty among the tenors, which in turn affected the contraltos. As Graham removed his hands and feet from the organ, he indulged in a loud sigh which echoed around the chancel. I waited for a minute or so before reading the prayers for the welfare of the borough and the guidance of the council and its figurehead.

When I ascended the pulpit to the uninhibited strains of 'Praise My Soul the King of Heaven', I surveyed the congregation. It was a motley throng. The political elite of the borough occupied the first three rows on either side of the aisle. Behind them were ranged on the left-hand side the Cubs and Scouts of the parish and on the right-hand side the immaculately arrayed Guides, with the scowling-faced Captain at the end of the pew. In the rest of the full church were members of the Sunday congregation, some of whom had brought their friends. Together with them were those who had come out of curiosity after reading the announcement of the service in the local press, representing which was Ed Jenkins, peering up at me through his rimless spectacles. As I spotted him with his pencil raised and his note pad ready, I made a mental note to keep a rein on my tongue after giving out my text, 'Our citizenship is in heaven'.

'With this text, I suppose, I could combine one from the Sermon on the Mount: "You cannot serve God and Mammon",' I said. 'Our new Mayor has demonstrated the truth of those words by his fearless onslaught on corruption in council circles in the not too distant past. I am sure that his term of office will be marked by a devotion to the highest principles in civic administration.

'Nothing is more important than the trust the citizens of Abergelly should have in their elected representative,' I went on. 'They want to know that the money they pay in rates is spent wisely and responsibly.' The Mayor was nodding his head vigorously. 'The aims we heard announced in the mayoral address yesterday of good education in our schools, cleanliness in our streets, the upgrading of our council houses, will all require careful husbandry by the councillors but, above all, by the officials who are employed by them.'

The Mayor's head remained still, his brow furrowed. Evidently he was pondering what I was about to say next. So was Ed Jenkins, his pencil held aloft. 'To use a well-known cliché, Rome was not built in a day,' I said.

Then it happened! There was a shout from the back of the church. 'This isn't a sermon! It's a political speech.'

This was followed by the banging of a coin on the back of the pew. By now the man was standing, pointing his finger at me. It was Joe Roberts, pastor of an independent chapel in the downtown area of Abergelly.

'Preach the gospel, man! That's what you are paid to do!'

I stood speechless. It was not an occasion for a dialogue. 'And now to God the Father, the Son and the Holy Spirit, be all honour and glory,' I intoned. 'Hymn number 196.'

I came down from the pulpit in a silence which would have done justice to a Trappist monastery. As the organist thundered the opening notes of the hymn, the bewildered congregation rose to their feet with their heads turned to the back of the church instead of being bowed over their hymn books. I doubt if 'Guide Me, O Thou Great Redeemer' has ever been sung in Wales with such a lack of passion.

No sooner had I finished the vestry prayer than the door burst open and Joe Roberts confronted me. He was a little man, barely five foot tall. He dug his finger in my chest. 'That was not worthy of a man of the cloth,' he hissed in front of the fascinated audience of the Abergelly church choir.

'Before you go any further, Mr Roberts,' I managed to say, with great difficulty containing my wrath, 'if you had had the humility to listen to the whole of my sermon you would have heard the gospel expounded. As it is, you have deprived the congregation of the opportunity to hear it. Will you please leave this church immediately before I have you arrested for a breach of the peace?' I pointed my finger towards the door in a dramatic gesture which mirrored his intrusion into my sermon, but with much greater effect. He turned on his heels as the choir made a way for him to go out into the churchyard.

When I returned to the church to escort the Mayor and the council from their pews, I found myself in the middle of what Joe Roberts would describe as political mayhem. The contingent had been joined by Ed Jenkins, eager to employ his pencil and pad.

'I am very sorry, Mr Mayor,' I said, 'for that unwarranted interruption in the service. I have told the intruder that he was in danger of arrest for a breach of the peace.'

'He certainly was,' announced the Town Clerk. 'It is unfortunate that the Chief Constable was not able to be present, otherwise there could have been an arrest.'

'I wouldn't have wanted that,' said the Mayor. 'The best thing is to pretend that it never happened.'

With the local reporter in attendance, this was a wish that could not be fulfilled. Ed Jenkins could see tomorrow's headlines splashed across the *Monmouthshire Gazette*. Once again, despite my best endeavours, my sermon would provide red hot copy for the local press. In Eleanor's words, 'You must be a Godsend to them after your predecessor. The only time he appeared in their columns was as a result of taking weddings and funerals. That was in small print, of course.'

As we sat in the front room of the Vicarage, the Mayor suggested that perhaps it would have been wiser for me to stay in the pulpit and to wait until the protester had finished his dictate. Already he was on his third tumbler of whisky.

'My dear Mr Mayor,' I replied, emboldened by my second tumbler, 'that man would have ranted on until Doomsday. I was taught in my theological college by the warden, who is now a bishop, that once you are in the pulpit and your congregation's attention has either waned through boredom or occasionally has been distracted by some unexpected occurrence, the wisest course is to shut up and come down. I am sure that I did the right thing. Of course,' I added, 'I could have called on the people's warden from St David's to remove the man. Since he is well over six feet, with the physique of an ox, and a second-row forward, he could have carried the five-foot Joe Roberts with one arm and deposited him outside the church. I think that of all the alternatives, my actions this morning were the best under the circumstances.'

To my astonishment the Town Clerk applauded my decision to come down from the pulpit. 'I must agree, Mr Mayor,' he said. 'It was an unseemly, very unseemly episode, which could have become even more unseemly. I am sure that the Chaplain's course of action was the only means of minimizing what could have been a most unpleasant scene.' He sat back and swallowed a glass of gin and tonic, having delivered the final word.

From then on the conversation turned to other matters, and it was in danger of petering out when Mrs Cooper knocked the door to inform us that the Mayor's car had come, 'but he'll wait until his worship is ready'. It was with great relief that Eleanor and I waved them goodbye on the Vicarage doorstep and went into the dining room, where the smell of roast beef met us in all its fullness after the hints of its readiness had percolated into the front room.

During the meal, Elspeth wanted to know why 'that naughty man' had shouted at her daddy. Once again David hastened to supply the answer, as a uniformed member of the Scout organization. 'Akela told us that we mustn't be afraid of the row, cos we all were, and said that the man was most likely out of his mind and didn't know what he was talking about. Were you afraid, Elspeth?'

'Yeth,' she said. 'I held Mammy's hand very tight, didn't I, Mam?'

'You did indeed,' she replied. 'Now then, shall we all start to eat this lovely dinner that Auntie Cooper has cooked for us?' Silence descended on the dinner table. As my sister used to recite in 'The Old Welsh Maid', a sketch about Welsh courtship where the despairing maiden had waited many years for a proposal which never came, 'He was only there for the food. No talking, only eating.'

Later on that afternoon, there was a telephone call as I relaxed in the study. As soon as I picked up the receiver, my heart sank. The unmistakable high-pitched tones of Ed Jenkins assaulted my eardrums.

'Sorry to trouble you, Vicar. This is Ed Jenkins here, especially on a Sunday, but could I come round now in the next half hour or so, about the, er, how shall we call it, the, er, dramatic incident in this morning's service? You see, I want to get the report in tomorrow's edition.'

I paused and then sighed as loudly as the organist's verdict on that morning's anthem. 'Very well, Mr Jenkins, but you must realize that a Sunday afternoon is a vicar's oasis in a busy day.'

'Sorry, Vicar,' he said. 'I promise I won't keep you more than a few minutes.'

'I've heard that before,' I replied. 'However, if you come now, immediately, you will be able to catch me before I fall asleep.'

In the space of a few minutes there was a ring at the doorbell. 'Don't bother, Mrs Cooper,' I shouted, 'I'll answer it.'

The indefatigable news reporter was facing me with the light of battle gleaming in his bespectacled, beady eyes. 'Just a moment or so,' he assured me. I took him into my study.

'Well, all I want to know, Vicar,' he breathed, 'is why you did not have that man removed after his verbal attack, shall we say, this morning?'

'The answer to that, Mr Jenkins,' I replied, 'is that such a violent reaction would have been the very thing that he would have wanted, a martyrdom in the name of his Lord and Saviour. I told him in the vestry after the service that if he wanted a sermon he would have had it, following my introductory remarks.'

'Is there any chance of having your script, as it were?' enquired Ed Jenkins.

'I am afraid not,' I replied. 'As you should know by now, I preach without notes. However, I can assure you that if I had had a brain scan it would have revealed the kind of gospel message which the Reverend Joe Roberts would have appreciated, but he jumped the gun. That is fatal!'

# 9

When I went to visit Tom Beynon in hospital in late afternoon next day, he was sitting up reading the evening newspaper. 'We've just had the *Gazette* delivered,' he told me.
'You've hit the headlines again! What a to-do! My missus
told me all about it when she came in last night. I wish I'd
been there. I was in school with Joe Roberts – dull as a
brush. Good rugby player for the school, and that's about
it. How on earth he's become a minister, God knows. Mind,
I doubt if he's got more than a dozen people coming to his
tabernacle. I expect they're all as dull as he is. Anyhow,
they've certainly had publicity today. I see the Town Clerk
said that he could have been arrested. That's just what Joe
would have liked – to become a martyr for the cause. So it's
a good thing it didn't happen. Anyway, Vicar, good news.
I'm coming home tomorrow, so expect to see me in church
next Sunday. Mind, I'll be on crutches, but what does that
matter? I've missed being at St Peter's more than I can say.'

When he had finished this monologue, I told him that I
had received a letter from the Archdeacon that morning,
requesting the preparation of all the yearly statistics,
financial and otherwise, for his visitation in the deanery
next month.

'I tell you what,' commented the people's warden, 'he won't have anything to beat those figures in the rest of our deanery. Thank God he's not coming to our church to trip over the carpet, as he did last year, so he can't have any complaint on that account. I'm sure he thinks that we arranged to do that on purpose, judging by his attitude afterwards.'

'All I can say, Tom,' I replied, 'is that we have been in his black books ever since.'

'What is the betting,' said Eleanor at lunch, 'that our dear Miss Lewis will have informed him about the omission of the Easter offering in the annual accounts? As the daughter of the vicarage, she knows the procedure involved in the visitation.'

'In that case,' I replied, 'why haven't I heard from him by now?'

'Knowing our dear trinitarian friend,' she went on, 'he would much prefer to spring it on you at the annual set piece when you would be unprepared to defend yourself.'

'Thanks for the warning, my love,' I said. 'With an age-long tradition behind me, I shall be able to turn the tables on him if he seeks to imply that I have been trying to pull a fast one. Backed up as I shall be by my church officers, I shall be only too pleased to refer to them for support. Tom Beynon will be the first to put down the mighty from his seat.'

'I don't think that he will accuse you of double dealing,' she replied, 'but he will be able to suggest that you should have known that the Easter offering ought to have been included in the accounts. After all, when you were Vicar of Pontywen, your annual bonus was always recorded in the accounts. I'll tell you one thing,' she said, 'from now on, ancient tradition or not, that money will be in the form of a cheque and not cash counted in the Vicarage on Easter Day.'

On the Thursday of that week, I was due to perform my first dedication as Mayor's Chaplain at the newly built nursery school in the more affluent district of the town. As Eleanor said, this innovation would have been more appropriate in our own Brynfelin, where the only nursery for the three- or four-year-olds was the council house which was their home. Her opinion was echoed by Hugh Thomas after Matins on Thursday morning. As someone who would be a parent in the not too distant future, he was extremely sarcastic.

'Surely, Vicar,' he said, 'you will feel more than a little out of place saying prayers over something where the ratepayers' money would have been better spent in your own parish? I'm glad I am not a Mayor's chaplain.'

'My dear Hugh,' I replied, 'with your past record of the last few months I don't think there will be much prospect of that in the near future.' His face reddened and he left the vestry without another word.

It was a bright but blustery day when I arrived in my Ford at the Pengarth Nursery School, an ugly prefabricated structure, erected at the minimum cost, by the look of it. There was a gathering of well-dressed ladies and a number of equally well-dressed gentlemen outside. Inside the school, with its large double-glazed windows, I could see the young infants in the company of their teachers. My car suffered comparison with its fellow vehicles. At the moment the mayoral car was conspicuous by its absence.

I collected my robes and my prayer book and joined the chattering elite.

For a valley function it was atypical, to say the least. As I drew close to two ladies in tweeds, the one lady was asking her companion, 'Have you heard or seen the willow warbler yet? It seems to be late this year.' The other tweeded counterpart replied, 'I haven't, but my cousin in Builth Wells said she heard it in the woods behind her house last week. So I expect it will be with us very soon now.'

When they saw me they came up to me and gushed, 'Good morning, Vicar! What a lovely day.' The elder of the two introduced herself. 'I am Philippa Bartholomew Davies, of Basildon Court, and this is my friend Emma Brandon Lewis, my neighbour. How wonderful that our family educational trust has been able to finance this educational experiment in Abergelly. It is so important that the education of the, er, working classes begins at the earliest possible age.'

My hackles shot up at this comment. As a product of the working classes myself, I found it insulting to be treated as less than the dust, some inferior layer of human society in need of assistance by the upper reaches who had condescended to stoop down to help.

'May I say, ladies,' I managed to say, finding it difficult to control my tongue, 'that as a member of the working classes, I am grateful to my parents for the education they gave me until I was old enough to go to infant school. They were intelligent and literate. I should imagine that the parents of the young children coming to this school in such a prosperous part of Abergelly are as competent as my parents to give their offspring a good education in these very early years. Where education at such a tender age is necessary is in the council house limbo, where nothing has been done to care for those children in families who have been dumped in a so-called development area such as Brynfelin in my parish. The bulk of those parents are not of the highest intelligence and are therefore incapable of providing their children with the kind of upbringing which will fit them for the infant school. Many of them will not be able to read or count. I must apologize for this outburst, but I can assure you, ladies, it comes from my soul.'

To say that they were startled at my tirade would be an understatement. 'Excuse me, I must have a word with my brother,' said Philippa B.D. 'Are you coming, Emma?' Emma B.L. was only too pleased to accept the invitation.

It was then that the mayoral car came into sight, bearing the Mayor and Mayoress, plus the Chairman of the Education Committee, Llew Williams, and his wife, commonly known as Bella Bull's Eye because she had been the champion of the Ladies' League Darts Team over the past twenty years, although my wife very unkindly suggested that it might be due to her unprepossessing appearance. I came to greet them with a sense of overwhelming relief.

'I didn't know that this was a private endeavour,' I remarked to Llew.

'Well, let me put it this way,' he replied. 'If it is something that we can't afford, let that lot pay for it, especially since they have agreed to pay towards its upkeep. It will be their pet scheme.'

'I'm afraid I have offended two of the aristocratic ladies by objecting to their use of the word "working class",' I said. 'I told them that this nursery school would be of much more use in Brynfelin than down here in the more well-to-do part of Abergelly.'

'Quite right, Vicar,' he replied, 'but let me give you a tip. Keep out of politics, as that nut head shouted last Sunday. Your job is to say the prayers. Leave it at that and you'll be all right.'

With my ego punctured I went into the school and enquired of one of the teachers where I could robe for the ceremony. She led me into their rest room, primitively furnished with a few armchairs and the minimum amount of accessories. As I was donning my cassock, a tall thin lady came into the room. She had a bony face which matched her body. Her sparse hair had been pulled back into a bun which seemed to bristle with more hair pins than hair. She was a lady in her early fifties, it would appear. 'Stephanie Arnold, head of this nursery school.'

'I am Fred Secombe, Vicar of Abergelly,' I replied. 'Quite frankly, I wish I were dedicating this school in my own parish on the new housing estate which has sprung up on the hill which overlooks the town.'

'Very poetic, Vicar,' she retorted in dry, sarcastic tones, 'but as you know, beggars can't be choosers. Perhaps one day your parish will be blessed with something similar, probably even more advanced than this somewhat primitive building, if one may call it that. I have no illusions about the Pengarth Nursery School at the moment. I can only hope that over the next few years we shall be blessed by an increase in the number of educational aids which are necessary to the development of these very young children. Now that we have been quite open in our approach to each other, shall we shake hands?'

'By all means, Stephanie,' I said, 'if I may call you that.'

'By all means, Fred,' she replied. 'Now I shall let you put on your clerical equipment in peace.'

As she left the room, I wondered why I had ignored the advice of the Chairman of the Education Committee by entering the field of local politics at the earliest opportunity. The only consolation I found on reflection was that I was aware that the pivotal figure in the experiment was not a cipher but someone who was concerned about the plight of the disadvantaged young children.

I dressed myself and went out into the crowd which surrounded the entrance to the school. The Mayor, whose breath was overladen with his favourite brand of spirit which was stocked in abundance in the Mayor's Parlour, was engaged in conversation with Colonel Brendan Phillips, Chairman of the Trust. 'Ah, the Mayor's Chaplain!' he exclaimed. 'Colonel, meet my dear friend and my chaplain! Harry Secombe's elder brother.'

'I beg your pardon, Mr Mayor, I am Fred Secombe,' I interrupted. 'My name is Fred Secombe and I am Vicar of Abergelly.'

'Good for you, Vicar,' said the Colonel. 'How should you be known as somebody else's brother? I suffered from that when I was at Eton, where my elder brother was head of the house, captain of the cricket team and God knows what else. It has taken me thirty years to be known as myself.' Suddenly I felt at home, far removed from the bird-watching duo who had goaded me into my intemperate invective earlier on.

The Mayor stood undecided what to do next, like the opposition member of parliament described by Lloyd

George so many years ago as someone sitting on the fence for so long that iron had entered into his soul. He was saved by Stephanie Arnold, who emerged from the school with the announcement that everything was ready for the ceremony.

After I had read the appropriate prayers, the Mayor proclaimed that the school was now officially opened, after a third tug at curtains veiling the commemorative tablet. A pretty little blonde stepped forward and, with a carefully rehearsed curtsey, presented a bouquet of spring flowers to the Mayoress. Blodwen Stewart, in her Marks and Spencer twin set adorned with her chain of office, gathered up the child in her arms and smothered her with kisses, despite the impediment of having one hand clutching the floral tribute. Everybody clapped gently but not enthusiastically, and the opening ritual was over.

After we had been escorted around the small building with its array of building bricks, slides, dolls' houses and a small sand pit, we were invited into the rest room for coffee and biscuits. Philippa and Emma confined themselves to one corner of the room as far removed from me as possible. The Chairman of the Trust forgot his sympathy for my position as an elder brother and plied me with questions about Harry. The Mayor betrayed signs of impatience on discovering that the only means of refreshment was non-alcoholic, and it was not long before the experiment in nursery school education was left in peace. I waited until the last expensive car glided out of the makeshift car park and my Ford had a clear run into the open. As my wife had informed me on numerous occasions, I was unable to park a car: I always abandoned it, according to her. At least I had a warm farewell as I drove away from the Pengarth Nursery School, with the children waving.

By now the wind had died down and it was gloriously sunny. I had an hour to spare before lunchtime. The mountains beckoned to me, so I pointed my car in that direction. Halfway up Llanaber mountain, my recently purchased saloon car began to suffer from the strain of the very steep climb. Steam appeared from the bonnet. I pulled in to the side of the road and switched off the engine. There were no dwellings in that inhospitable region, nor was there much prospect of passing traffic.

I waited until the last vestige of steam had vanished. It was the first time that I had had occasion to open the bonnet. I spent many minutes investigating where the open sesame was placed on the dashboard. The heat was intense when I succeeded in exposing the inner workings of the vehicle to the mountain air.

Once again I waited quite a while before daring to remove the radiator cap with a filthy-looking rag I found in the boot. I unscrewed the red hot top, almost blistering my fingers in the process, and averted my face as a column of steam, apparently from the bowels of hell, rocketed into the sky.

For the third time I waited, sprawled out on the heathered slope and developing a tan to compensate for my misfortune. Not a car nor a lorry chose to come my way. As I lay in a state of complete abandon, I recalled that I had not put any water into the radiator since the day of purchase. I could see my wife's face when I would have to reveal the result of my neglect, and it was not at all comforting.

Then suddenly the stillness was broken by the sound of a heavy lorry crawling up the mountain. I went to the middle of the road and stood as the National Coal Board lorry came into view, groaning under its heavy load of anthracite. I was determined to stop it at all costs. One thing was certain. It could not run me over at that speed.

It took an age to reach me. As the driver applied his brakes, his mate jumped down from the cabin and came to meet me. 'Trouble?' he enquired, obviously a man of few words. Had I not been a man of the cloth, I could have provided a suitable retort.

'My radiator's completely dry,' I said.

'Leak, is it?' he asked, using two more words than his first enquiry.

'I have no idea,' I replied. 'All I know is that I shall have to get some water from somewhere. I don't suppose you have any water on board your lorry?'

He stared at me. 'No,' he said.

By now the driver had climbed down and came to join in the conversation. 'The Vicar's car 'ave broken down,' said the mate to the driver.

'I can see that, you dull bugger,' came the reply. 'What can I do for you, Vicar?' he went on. 'Looks like a blown gasket or something like that. I can give you a tow over the hill to Evans' Garage on the other side. How are your brakes?'

'Excellent,' I assured him.

'I ask about your brakes,' he said, 'because of going down the other side of the mountain. I can pull you up to the top quite safely, but once we get down the other side you'll 'ave to keep your foot on the brake all the way to the garage. Right! Let's get the two ropes out, 'Arry.'

No sooner had he said this than we heard the unmistakable roar of a powerful saloon car's engine as it made light of the gradient facing it. In seconds a Jaguar rolled up behind the lorry. To my astonishment, Colonel Brendan Phillips joined the trio. 'You're off course, Vicar,' he said, 'and evidently in need of assistance.'

Somewhat resentfully, the working-class lorry driver told him, 'We're going to give 'is reverence a tow.'

'But, my dear man,' remonstrated the Colonel, 'how in God's name is the Vicar going to get down the hill on the other side? It will be a suicidal exercise. What exactly is the matter, Vicar?'

'I'm afraid my radiator steamed up and is completely dry,' I replied.

'Might I suggest that I go down to the garage at the bottom of the hill and bring some water to refill your radiator, then you can drive down and let the garage people see to your car, and they can tell you whether it is something serious or not?'

I thanked him profusely for his kindness, then I turned to the servant of the National Coal Board to thank him, but he had gone back to his cab. He revved up his engine, his eyes on the road, ignoring me. I waved my gratitude as his monster groaned its way. It was a pointless gesture.

'Now then, Vicar,' said the Colonel, 'you stay here with your vehicle. I shall be back in a jiffy.'

True to his word, his jiffy was no more than ten minutes. By now the radiator was able to receive the water without a murmur of protest. I screwed on the top and went to the driving seat, saying a short prayer. I switched on the ignition, put my foot on the accelerator and the music of my Ford engine had never sounded so sweet. My rescuer opened the car door. 'Nothing much wrong with that,' he declared. 'I have put the empty cans in your boot. Safe journey back to your Vicarage.'

'I can't thank you enough,' I told him.

'Always a pleasure to help a man of the cloth,' he replied, using the phrase of Joe Roberts, man of God and working-class minister of a back-street chapel in Abergelly.

When I drove into Evans' Garage, I was met by a gentleman from behind the desk in the office, evidently the owner.

'Colonel Phillips said you would be bringing the car back and that you would like us to see if it is all right,' he said. I gave him his cans and waited in his office while my Ford was examined. After a quarter of an hour or so, he came back into the office. 'Everything seems to be in order,' was the verdict.

'I have a confession to make,' I said.

'I thought we were the ones to make a confession,' he replied.

'We are all sinners,' I retorted. 'Anyway, I have to admit that I have not checked the radiator since I bought the car some months ago.'

'Isn't it nice to be able to lecture a priest and tell him not to do that again!' said Mr Edgar Evans, the proprietor. 'But, believe me, it is a very important lecture if you want to hang on to your car.'

'How much do I owe you?' I asked.

'It's enough to have the pleasure of giving a sermon to a vicar,' came the reply. He shook my hand and I drove out of the petrol station to face another sermon from my wife.

'You are late,' she said, when I pulled up outside the Vicarage door.

'It's a long story but it will wait until after lunch,' I replied.

'That means that you have been in trouble,' she said.

'Funnily enough,' I remarked, 'that is the word the National Coal Board employee used to me.'

Once the children had gone to school my wife joined me in the sitting room for a postprandial drink. As we sat opposite each other in our armchairs, she said, 'Now that we are sitting comfortably, you can begin.' She listened with much amusement until I arrived at the saga of the boiling radiator.

'Secombe!' she exploded. 'I know that you would make the world's worst mechanic, but even you must realize you have to keep a check on the water in your radiator. From now on, I shall remind you constantly to do that. The Colonel must have thought that you and common sense were strangers to each other. Speaking of which, Willie James called while you were being rescued by the gallant soldier. He would not tell me the purpose of his visit, but you will be pleased to know that you will be graced by his presence at seven o'clock this evening.'

'That's all I need to round off an exciting day,' I said. 'I wonder what triviality he will bring to my attention as something verging on a crisis of great magnitude. In the meanwhile I think I shall call in at Abergelly Secondary Modern to have a word with Ivor Hodges and to let him know that Tom Beynon will be back in action next Sunday, albeit with a stick and a leg in plaster. He will be greatly relieved to know that he can be back in the bell tower before the service, instead of covering for his fellow warden downstairs.'

'You can say that again,' replied Eleanor. 'Those bells are like children to him, especially since he has no family, and I must say he has done wonders in that belfry. When we came here first the invitation to worship was confined to a few discordant clangs and not the impressive cascade of notes we have today. All that in the space of a few years! I know you think the world of our friend Tom, but Ivor has been an even greater friend to you in some ways. You are lucky to have two men like that.'

Ivor was surprised to see me. 'Trouble at mill?' he asked.

'Don't mention that word to me,' I said fiercely. 'I have had enough of that for today. As far as you are concerned, I think you will consider my news a cause for relief. Tom Beynon will be on duty next Sunday despite the handicap of a leg in plaster. He is so desperate to be back in harness that I think he could have been wheeled into St Peter's on his hospital bed. So I bring you the good tidings that you can be up in the bell tower on Sunday morning.'

'Thank God for that,' he replied. 'I shall be able to get them to sharpen up Friday night's practice. Last Sunday morning's shambles was purgatory for me as I stood at my post in the nave, listening to a cacophony which was supposed to be a tuneful call to worship. It will be good to have Tom back with us. That man is a gem. I don't think he has any ill will to anybody, unlike our dear Miss Lewis.'

'Oh, no!' I exclaimed. 'What have you heard about her?'

'A friend of mine is Harry Evans,' he went on, 'who is the head at Cwmllew Grammar School. He is also Chairman of the Scouts Association for this neck of the woods. Apparently she has written to him suggesting that Willie James is incapable of being a Scout leader and that his Scouts are ill-disciplined and a bad advertisement for the Scout movement. She goes on to say that her Guides have been harassed by the boys at church parades. She claims that she has written to him because the Vicar ignores the situation. He rang me this morning when he received the letter, asking me to let you know and that he would be in touch with you in the next few days.'

'So that's why little Willie is coming to see me this evening,' I remarked. 'This, indeed, is trouble at mill. I know that he is not another Baden-Powell, by any means, but he is dedicated to the movement and in his limited way he does his best. 'Tis a poor thing, but mine own.' He has been in charge of those boys for the past ten years. It is his life. After I have heard what he has to say this evening, tomorrow I shall pay a visit to Miss Lewis. I don't think she realizes that in taking this action without consulting me she is in grave danger of losing her own position as Guide Captain.'

Ivor's face broke into a smile. 'I shall follow these events with interest,' he said.

Eleanor was incensed at the news when she returned from her clinic. 'The sooner that woman takes her custom elsewhere, the better,' she spluttered in her wrath. 'A fine vicar's daughter she is. I bet her poor father must have suffered from her attentions. Can you imagine what would have happened if she had been elected to the Parochial Church Council? You must do all you can to boost the morale of Willie when he comes this evening.'

'You needn't tell me that, my dear,' I replied. 'He will have grown a few more inches by the time he leaves the Vicarage, believe me. I know he has ideas above his station and, should I say, his height, but at least he is a dedicated churchman. I don't want him hurt by an insensitive drag- on of a woman.'

'Hold on,' interrupted my wife. 'You are beginning to sound like a male chauvinist. It was just an accident of birth that created the dragon. It could have been male or female. The result would have been exactly the same, a blot on society.'

With those words we turned to our evening meal.

'Daddy,' asked Elspeth, 'what doth a dragon look like?'

'You know,' explained David, 'it has got big jaws, a long body and a very long tail, and it's got scaly skin and it's red and it can breathe fire.'

'Very good description,' said his mother.

'But who ith the dragon? Who ith going to hurt Mr James?' enquired my daughter. 'He'th thuch a little man and he'll be gobbled all up.'

'My dear Elspeth,' I told her, 'those are different kinds of dragons. There are the ones like David described, and there are other ones who pretend to be people. They don't gobble people up. They just hurt them very much. They are not nice. We were talking about one of those. Now you go off and read your books and forget about dragons.'

Promptly at seven o'clock, Willie James rang the door-bell. He appeared very agitated.

'Come on in, Willie,' I said warmly. We went into my study where I made a great fuss of ushering him into an armchair and offering him a drink.

'If you don't mind, Vicar, I won't have anything. I want to keep a cool head.'

'This sounds serious, Willie,' I said. 'Well, sit down and let's hear the whole story, whatever it is.' As I looked at the little figure swallowed up by the armchair, I felt a strong urge to take Miss Lewis apart when I next met her and to do to her what she was attempting to do to poor Willie.

'I'm sorry to trouble you, Vicar,' he began, 'but last night in the church hall was the Scouts' night, as you know. Well, I was just beginning a talk on orienteering when the Guide Captain came in with some of her Guides. Their night is on Thursday, as you also know. I asked her what she was doing, coming in on our night. She said that those six girls had to take part in a Guide competition on Saturday and she was giving them extra instruction. When I said why didn't she do that on Thursday, she told me to mind my own business.

'By now the boys were getting restless. "Look at them," she said, "no discipline at all. I have written to the Chairman of the Scouts' Association about you and your so-called Scout troop. You will be hearing from him very shortly I expect."

'Vicar, I felt terrible. There she was, in front of my Scouts, calling us names and heaven knows what. Fair play to the boys, once she had gone they told me not to worry and that they would say to the Chairman that we had the best troop in our district. I try to do my best, Vicar. That's all I can do. Nobody can do more than his best.'

By now I had come to the irrevocable decision that Miss Lewis would have to surrender her post as Guide Captain. Not only that, but it was heartening to hear that Willie's troop was so supportive, even if undisciplined.

'All I can say, Willie, is this,' I told him. 'You have my full support. If the Chairman of the Scouts Association contacts me, I shall say the same to him. In that case, nothing that Miss Lewis has said will affect your position as Scout leader. It is a church organization and the incumbent is responsible for the appointment.'

His face relaxed and there was a sign of a smile; perhaps 'glimmer' would be more exact. 'I think I will have that drink now, Vicar,' he said. 'A beer, if you've got one.' As he swallowed a sample of the local ale, Willie became his jaunty self once again. 'Is there any chance of me doing Pooh-Bah in *The Mikado*?' he asked.

## 10

Cartref, St Leger Crescent, was an Edwardian house, three up and three down, two streets away from St Peter's Church in a respectable neighbourhood, the preserve of bank clerks, school teachers, works foremen and the equivalent. It was the newly acquired house of Miss Edwina Lewis, who had acquired the reputation of a formidable figure, physically and otherwise, in the space of six months. Warned by my wife that I should not enter the den of the lioness, I ignored her advice and rang the doorbell the next evening after Willie's visit to the Vicarage. It had a loud, strident tone, calculated to put the fear of God into anyone who dared to cross the threshold. Already I was beginning to rue my foolhardiness.

I was about to move from the doorstep, congratulating myself on a lucky escape, when the door was flung open. 'Oh! It's you,' she exclaimed. There was no 'Vicar' in her acknowledgement of my presence, and the expression on her face was indicative of open hostility. It was not the most propitious start for what was going to be a painful interview in any case.

'I wonder if I might have a few words with you, Miss Lewis,' I managed to say in my best Rural Dean voice.

She looked at me suspiciously, evidently connecting my visit with her letter to the Scouts Association Chairman. 'Come on in,' she ordered.

I was shown into the front room, which reeked of furniture polish. The word *cartref* is 'home' in the Welsh language. Anything less like a home than this cheerless space it would be difficult to find. The sole decorations on the walls were certificates of various kinds. There was a leather-covered three-piece suite, defying any visitor to dull its shine by sitting in it. A small table occupied the centre of the floor, devoid of a flower pot or any form of adornment – a doctor's surgery would have had some magazines on the table at least. As Tom Beynon would have said, it had no soul.

'Do you mind if I sit down?' I asked.

'If you want to,' she replied. She stayed standing for a second or two. Then she decided to sit down opposite me in the other armchair. 'Well,' she demanded, 'what is this visit all about?'

'Miss Lewis,' I began, 'I understand that you have written to the Chairman of the Scouts Association, suggesting that Willie James should be sacked from his position as Scout leader because of his incompetence. Furthermore, you included me in your missive, stating that I ignored his inability to control his Scouts.'

Her face reddened but her eyes blazed. 'It's true, isn't it?' she replied in a loud voice. 'Surely to goodness you realize that the man is incapable of maintaining any kind of discipline. Unless something is done about it, your Scouts will become the laughing stock of the valley, if they aren't already. I'll tell you what, my Guides would not dare to put a foot out of step.'

I swallowed hard. 'I have come to inform you, Miss Lewis, that they are not your Guides from now on. I am afraid that I cannot countenance your interference in parochial matters any longer. You wrote to the Archdeacon about the Easter offering, you flounced out of the Easter Vestry meeting when you were not proposed for the Parochial Church Council. Now you have interfered with a matter which is none of your business. Under those circumstances I have no alternative but to ask you to step down from your position as Guide Captain.'

As her complexion changed from red to deep purple, I feared for a moment that she was about to suffer a stroke. There was a pause. Then words gushed from her in a vituperative torrent as she stood up and looked down on me.

'I don't believe it! You have the cheek to attack me for drawing attention to your illegal cover-up of your Easter offering. Then you object to me bringing the utter incompetence of your so-called Scoutmaster to the notice of the Scout Movement. If you had more control of your parish, these things would not have happened. I tell you what, my father had more control in his parish than you will ever have. How in God's name you were appointed Rural Dean I'll never know. And I'll tell you something else, I shall not darken the doors of your parish church ever again. I would rather drive miles to another church than to walk the few yards to St Peter's.'

It was my turn to stand up. 'Good evening, Miss Lewis,' I said with all the dignity I could put into those words. Then I moved towards the door rapidly.

She moved even more rapidly and stood between me

and the door. 'Don't you dare go until I have finished my piece,' she snarled.

I had no desire to indulge in a physical encounter with the virago. In any case, her sheer bulk would have made me the loser, but by now I was determined not to tolerate the onslaught any longer. 'Miss Lewis,' I said very loudly, 'you are not talking to your schoolchildren. You are talking to the vicar of the parish. I would have thought from your upbringing in a vicarage that you would have learned to have respect for the clergy. Evidently not. Now I should be much obliged if you would stand aside and let me see myself out of this house.'

I looked her straight in the eye. It was almost nose to nose. There followed an interminable pause, like the one between two tom cats in the garden prior to an outbreak of fighting. To my great relief, she moved out of the way and I was away from Cartref in a flash.

As I walked back to the Vicarage, I could imagine my wife telling me that a letter would have been preferable to a physical confrontation. 'I told you what would happen,' she would say. It was then that I had another physical confrontation of a more agreeable kind. Dai Elbow was about to open the Vicarage gates.

'I was just coming to see you, Vicar,' he said cheerily.

'Great to see you, Dai,' I replied heartily.

His smile broadened at my remark. 'If you can spare a few moments, I've got some ideas to raise money for St David's.'

'Wonderful,' I said. 'Come on in and tell me all about it.' I opened the front door and ushered the churchwarden into my study. 'Would you care for a beer, Dai?' I enquired.

'Beautiful,' he replied. As I went into the kitchen my wife appeared from the front room.

'Well, how did it go?' she asked.

'Dai Elbow is in the study,' I whispered. 'Tell you later.' She tried to read my face, but I had gone before she could have even a cursory study.

By the time I had produced two bottles of the local brew and opened them, my turbulence had subsided. 'Now then, Dai,' I said, 'let's have it.'

'Well, I've been thinking,' he began, with an air of importance. 'We've got an 'uge task in front of us if we're going to get the money for building the church. There's 'ardly any chance of the money coming from the collections. It's got to come from outside, right?' I nodded my head. 'Well, my first idea is to 'ave a charity rugby match. I know a lot of the old players, some of them internationals. The Curate knows loads of the blokes playing today. We could 'ave a Past versus Present match. The season's over now, but we could 'ave it next August before they start up again. That's the first. Wot do you think, Vicar?'

'Excellent,' I said. 'Have you had a word with Hugh Thomas about your idea?'

'I thought I'd come to you first, Vicar, but I know 'e'd be all for it. It would give 'im a chance of a game, wouldn't it? I'm sure 'e'd jump at it.'

'Maybe, Dai,' I replied, 'but don't forget that he will be well on the way to being a father by then. Suppose he gets hurt?'

'It's a friendly, Vicar. They'll see to it that he doesn't get 'urt. Now then, my second idea. Wot about a weekly or a monthly sweepstake? I could get all the local bookies to 'elp. Maybe some of the shops could sell tickets, and of course all the church people could do their bit by selling tickets to their neighbours and friends. After all, the Catholics do it, so why shouldn't we?'

'Hold on, Dai,' I interrupted. 'I'm afraid I can't see the bookies selling tickets for church funds, not under any circumstances. I know one of them had his daughter christened at St Peter's, but even he would draw the line at that. As far as the shops are concerned, I don't think they would sell tickets either. They might have a collecting tin on the counter, maybe. Anyway, that is not the way to raise money for the church.'

His face fell. 'All right then,' he went on, 'let's leave the bookies and the shops out of it. There's no reason why the congregation couldn't sell tickets for a draw. It would be a regular income. You think about it, Vic. Now then, my third idea is to write to all the big bosses in this part of the world asking for donations – really big ones, I mean. After all, if the Earl is going to give thousands of pounds and 'e doesn't even live 'ere, why can't they?'

'Now that's a good idea, Dai,' I replied. 'I must say, you must have been giving a lot of thought to ways and means of raising enough money to build our new church. We'll put these ideas to the Parochial Church Council's next meeting. Perhaps it will inspire some of them to think up new schemes.' The churchwarden of St David's glowed with pride. He had never been known as a master of originality. He felt that his hour had come.

After I had escorted him from the premises, I went into the front room where my wife turned off the television immediately and wanted a news report on my visit to Miss Edwina Lewis.

'All right,' I said. 'You win. I should have written a letter instead of entering her den. She was incensed at my cheek. Her father had more control of his parish than I would ever have. How in God's name I was appointed Rural Dean she would never know. Not only that, when I attempted to leave she stood between me and the door. "Don't you dare leave till I have finished my piece," she growled like a lioness. However, the best news is that she will never darken the doors of St Peter's ever again.'

'I knew this would happen,' replied my wife, 'but you wouldn't listen. That woman is more poisonous than Lucretia Borgia.'

'But, my dear,' I interrupted, 'if I wrote to her she would be on my doorstep in a flash. So the confrontation would be here. Home or away, it would not make much difference.'

'I suppose you are right,' she said. 'Well, what did Dai Elbow want? That was a long conversation.'

'Believe it or not,' I told her, 'he came with some ideas to raise money for the new church. A rugby match on the Abergelly ground between past players and present, a weekly sweepstake, and – this is the one worthwhile suggestion – that we should approach all the business magnates in the valley to see if their firms would give a large donation, using the Earl as the supreme example. Dai said he would approach the bookies to see if they would help with the sweepstake and that perhaps the shops would sell tickets. I told him that the idea of bookies selling tickets for the church was as far-fetched as the shopkeepers doing it.'

'Obviously,' said Eleanor, 'that is crazy, but a weekly sweepstake is not so crazy. The Roman Catholics use that money-making ploy quite effectively. I think his idea of involving the industrial concerns is an excellent one. As you say, it will need a lot of thought, but it could be most productive. Even the rugby match is a good idea. It will bring publicity to our cause, even if it does not raise much money. Our churchwarden is proving to be a real asset.'

'You should have seen him when I said that he had brought some good ideas,' I replied. 'The buttons nearly burst on his waistcoat!'

'Thank God there is always a Dai Elbow for every Edwina Lewis – probably a hundred Dai Elbows!' commented my wife.

The following Saturday was the Gilbert and Sullivan outing, eagerly anticipated by David and Elspeth, their first experience of joining a grown-up excursion to the seaside. There had been a great deal of debate about the venue. Eventually it was decided that this time our destination would be Barry Island instead of Porthcawl, mainly because of its larger funfair. Since there was a large number who wished to bring their boyfriends, wives and husbands, it meant that we had to order a double-decker bus from the United Valleys Company instead of from the local small-time operators. It was early June and we were blessed with a sunny, warm day. As Tom Beynon remarked, 'The Lord has chosen to compensate me for my fortnight in hospital, even if I can't go chasing the girls because of my crutches.'

'Fat lot of good it would do for you,' said his wife acidly. 'Even if you didn't have crutches, I don't think you would be able to catch a tortoise.'

There was the inevitable wait for latecomers as the bus stood outside the church hall. The driver began to complain that he would have to go before long because he had another appointment booked later in the morning. 'Always the same,' he muttered.

Ten minutes later three members of the male chorus arrived with their wives to complete the roster. 'We was 'aving a quick one in our 'ouse when we 'ad a shock when I looked at the clock,' said one poetically. To make up time we were given a rough ride through the valley route to the more civilized roads in the urban environment of Cardiff. David was beginning to look green by the time we reached Barry Island, but Elspeth seemed to revel in being shaken by the journey. 'It'th 'thiting,' she told her mother.

It was half past ten when we reached the big car park. Lunch had been arranged by Edna Evans, ticket secretary and member of the Parochial Church Council. She hassled everyone as they descended from the double-decker, reminding them of the time of lunch – one o'clock – and name of the restaurant, The Jolly Boys. Eleanor and I stood to one side as we listened to the monotonous chant of Edna as each excursionist left the bus.

'Now then,' said my wife to our two children, 'who wants to go bathing first, or who wants to go to the fair first?'

In unison they shouted, 'The fair!' I carried the holdall as we made our way through the big gates and into the pleasure palace. Elspeth was wide-eyed as she clutched her mother's hand and surveyed the delights surrounding her.

'What about a ride on one of those horses, like *The Magic Roundabout* on television?' asked Eleanor.

'Yeth pleathe!' she said fervently.

Then, turning around to David, who was walking with me scorning the offer of my hand, Eleanor asked, 'What about you, David?'

'That is for girls like Elspeth,' he replied scornfully. 'I want to go on one of those chairs that go up and over.'

My wife and I looked at each other. 'My dear David,' she said gently, 'you just about survived that bus ride. You were green. What do you think would happen to you if you went all those feet up into the air and came down like a bolt from the blue? Your stomach would turn over and you would be very sick.'

He looked down at the ground. Then he put on his big brother act and looked up at me. 'Well, Dad,' he said, 'perhaps I'd better keep Elspeth company. After all, she can't go up on that horse on her own.' A few minutes later the two of them were on the roundabout, with my son waving one arm about in the air, pretending to urge his steed faster by beating the animal with his hand.

Next we came to the coconut stand. 'Can I have a go, Dad?' he asked.

'I love coconutth,' said Elspeth, who had been given one by her uncle after he had opened a charity fair on one of his visits to South Wales. She had kept it on a shelf in her bedroom as if it were some kind of ornament. It was there for well-nigh twelve months before we disposed of it, not daring to crack it open. If we had done so, I am sure that it would not have been fit for human consumption.

After David had exhausted his bodily strength on a fruitless exercise, he challenged me to have a go. Basing my efforts on the hymn 'Thy Hand, O God, Hath Guided',

I was successful at the third time of asking. My prestige soared in the eyes of my son, and Elspeth was beside herself with joy at recovering her beloved ornament for the shelf, courtesy of her father instead of her uncle.

'It'th 'xactly the thame as Uncle Harry'th,' she said.

'Surprise, surprise,' murmured her mother.

By now, the two children were anxious to put on their bathing costumes. The sun was well up in the sky and the funfair was becoming claustrophobic.

As we ventured into the over-populated stretch of sand, I strove to find sufficient space to lay down the rug we had brought with us. My ears were assaulted by a familiar bellow. 'Vic, over by 'ere.' Dai Elbow was waving frantically some yards away.

After a safari which involved stumbling over bodies already victims to the solar rays, we reached the Abergelly Church Gilbert and Sullivan territory, marked out by bundles of clothes at regular intervals. Inside the confines of the corral were most of the busload. The majority of them were in their bathing costumes, including Willie James, whose puny physique was evidently suffering from its first contact with the bright sun.

'If I were you, Willie,' suggested my wife, 'I should smother my skin with a thick layer of suntan lotion, otherwise you could do yourself a nasty injury by the time the day is out. The alternative is to put your shirt on now before any more damage is done.' This was sufficient to send Willie scurrying to his clothes heap to retrieve a large bottle of lotion.

'Why on earth didn't you put that on before you started sunbathing?' asked Eleanor.

'I have very tough skin,' he replied.

'Whoever told you that was badly mistaken,' she said. 'I would say that you have very tender skin. Next time you sunbathe, protect it well before you lay it open to the sun's rays.'

We left the Scoutmaster using up his bottle and went to sit next to Hugh and Janet. Janet was wearing a voluminous cotton dress. 'Now then, young lady,' said my wife, 'would you like to get your hand in for the years to come by helping my daughter to get into her costume?'

'By all means,' she replied with a smile. 'It will be a pleasure.'

While Janet was engaged undressing Elspeth, Hugh said to me, 'I don't know if I am seeing things that are not there, but I get the feeling that Ivor Hodges is somewhat cool towards me. We sat next to him and his good lady in the bus, and the conversation was at a minimum. Mrs Hodges was fine and was chatting away to Janet, but he was hardly in a congenial mood. He spent most of his time looking out through the window. I don't think he smiled once during the journey.'

'I can't talk about it here, Hugh,' I replied, 'but when we meet on Monday morning I'll fill you in on one or two things. In the meanwhile, let's enjoy this lovely sunshine. It's not often that a seaside outing in this part of the world is blessed with weather like this.'

While Janet dealt with Elspeth, David had already donned his bathing trunks unaided. In the meanwhile Eleanor had changed into her costume after a number of manoeuvres involving towels. The sea appeared to be half swallowed by the sun and to be nearer Weston-Super-Mare than it was to South Wales.

'Well, Daddy,' demanded my wife, 'aren't you coming to watch us in the water?'

'Do you think we could hire a cab to get us there?' I said.

'The walk will do you good,' I was told. 'You don't get enough exercise these days. You'll soon be as obese as your brother if you're not careful.'

'God forbid,' I replied. 'All right, I'm coming.'

So we went down to meet the reluctant tide, I in my shirt and trousers and the rest of the family suitably clad for the occasion. My bathing expeditions were rare and certainly not during church outings.

'I don't know why you are so determined not to show your legs,' remarked my wife as we went on our safari. 'They are quite reasonable.'

'I may roll up my trouser legs whenever we get to the Bristol Channel,' I said, 'when they will be shown in part for a small fee.'

'Are we going to the Bristol Channel?' asked David.

'What'th a thmall fee?' enquired Elspeth.

By the time we had answered both questions, the tide had made up its mind to return to Barry. It was such a rapid *volte face* that I had no time to show off my legs or my feet. I was trapped with soaking shoes and socks, not to mention my trouser turn-ups, all to the great delight of my children and the helpless laughter of my wife.

'That will teach you not to come to the water's edge with clothing meant for pavements,' she said eventually.

I retired to a safe distance, removed my shoes and stockings, tucked up my trousers and stood and watched them as they splashed about in the somewhat murky water of the Bristol Channel, like three children let loose from servitude.

The staff of The Jolly Boys restaurant looked far from jolly as they strove to feed the hungry hordes invading their premises. Our company had booked tables for 67 according to Edna Evans. As one o'clock approached, there were still 13 places unfilled at our reserved benches. Our ticket secretary was in high dudgeon. She was a wisp of a woman in her late forties who took her duties far too seriously. Were it not for the excessive use of the raven colour dye which transformed the thin covering of hair surrounding her face, she could have played an old woman years ago, according to Tom Beynon.

'Lovely girl,' he told me, 'but a great worrier. No wonder she's got ulcers. She can hide her hair but she can't disguise her burps.' Already they were beginning to manifest themselves with a series of excuse-me's.

Suddenly an influx of miners, miners' wives and girlfriends produced an instant cure as she informed the hovering management that we had reached our 67 now. In no time at all plates of fish and chips were in front of us, with supplies of bread and butter to be fought over. The aroma of frying fat was intensified by the heat of the midday sun. To quote my sister's monologue once more, 'When her lover would come round in the evening at supper time, there was no talking, only eating.' All gossip ceased and food reigned supreme. There were several reinforcements of bread and butter, washed down with pop and tea. Plates of ice cream, liberally dosed with raspberry flavour, completed the meal.

When all had finished, Hugh Thomas, who had been elected as MC for the games in the afternoon, stood up and announced that we had to retire to the far end of the lawns, away from the funfair, where the festivities would be held.

'Only Tom Beynon and Elspeth will be exempt,' he said. 'Everybody else will have to take part when I say so. Age is no bar and condition is not to be counted, not even a bad elbow!' There was a roar of laughter.

Dai rose to his feet. 'May I say, Curate, that despite my elbow, I will try to do my best without 'urting a single soul in the competitions.'

On arrival at the chosen patch of green, away from the hoi polloi, Hugh proceeded to set up three wickets, plus bails, with a fourth wicket specially paced out at a distance of twenty-two feet. 'This match is going to be between the principals, stage helpers, musicians and box office staff plus their relatives and friends, and the chorus and their relatives and friends. Tom Beynon will be the umpire.'

'I thought you said I was going to be exempt,' objected Tom.

'What I meant was that you would not have to take an active part,' said my curate. 'You can sit in a deck chair at one end and we'll supply you with beer.'

'Under those conditions,' replied the churchwarden, 'I shall be pleased to act as umpire, and Elspeth can sit on my lap. By the way,' he went on, 'if we ever get through this lot it will be bad light stopped play!'

'You'll be surprised how quickly wickets will fall,' replied Hugh. 'I will be captain of the principals and Mr David Rees, churchwarden at Brynfelin, will be captain of the chorus. Come on, Dai, let's toss to decide who's batting first. When you have done that, you can write your batting order on those writing pads provided, plus pencil.'

The once-fit second-row forward, his abdomen dominating the top of his bathing trunks, strutted forward for the occasion. 'It's going to take 'alf an hour to write down all these names,' he said, 'especially the ones I can't spell. Well, 'ere goes.'

Tom Beynon tossed the coin, which landed in a thick clump of grass. After a search which refused to reveal its secret for a while until Dai claimed it to be in his favour, Hugh acknowledged defeat and his opponent surprisingly decided to bat last. There followed a huddle around Dai, who deputed Edna Evans to take down the names of his haphazardly chosen batting order. Meanwhile the Curate, with the scent of victory in his nostrils, had nominated the reluctant Ivor Hodges, opening batsman for the Abergelly second eleven, and the Vicar, a lower-order performer for the diocesan clergy team when in dire straits, as his leading batsmen.

'Come on Dai,' shouted the Curate. 'It's not the batting order at the moment, but your bowling selection you've got to decide.'

'That's what we're doing,' rejoined his churchwarden.

Ivor and I had to carve our way through the wall of human flesh to get to the wickets, the male contingent in a threatening inner ring with the female outskirts in knots of gossip. The opening bowler facing Ivor was the captain himself, the fearsome Dai Elbow. Behind the wickets was Willie James, who claimed to have played for the South Wales schoolboys' eleven.

Nearly two hours of mayhem later, it was decided to declare the result an honourable draw, with several minor casualties, about equal on either side, and with a unanimous desire to call it a day. After a brief consultation of the participants, all were of one mind that we spend the remaining hour in the spacious confines of the public bar on the sea front. Choruses of *The Pirates of Penzance* and *The Mikado* resounded, to the admiration of the customers at the Tivoli Hotel. Throughout all the noise, Elspeth slept soundly, clutching her coconut, while David strove manfully to keep awake to prove his male superiority.

At half past nine the double-decker bus drew up outside the church hall with a happy band of pilgrims. By now, Eleanor was carrying Elspeth and I had the more demanding task of transporting David. We made our way up the Vicarage drive.

Before we could open the front door, Mrs Cooper opened it for us in a state of great anxiety. 'The police 'ave been to see you, Vicar. Those vandals 'ave been at it again up in St David's. They've execrated the altar. The detective said they've painted sacrosanct words on the walls. He said he would be in touch with you in the morning.'

# 11

Once the children had been put to bed, I said to Eleanor, 'I can't wait until tomorrow morning, I must go up and see what damage has been done. I'll pick up Hugh on the way there.'

'It's just as well,' she replied, 'you would not be able to sleep otherwise. While you're up in Brynfelin, I'll get some supper ready.'

When I called at the Curate's house, Janet answered the door. 'You have heard about the break-in at St David's, then,' she said. 'The neighbours told us as soon as we got in from Barry Island. He's down at the church now.'

'Right,' I replied, 'I'll be with him straight away.'

The lights were all on when I arrived, illuminating a scene of chaos. Chairs were upturned, books were scattered over the floor. Most distressing was to see the altar frontal removed and bundled up in a heap which also contained the candlesticks, with the candles broken into pieces. There was no sign of the brass altar cross. Daubed on the walls were misspelt words like 'Holey Joes' and 'boddy eaters'. Standing in the middle of this devastation was a disconsolate Curate.

'Who on earth could have done this?' he said. 'Children would not have used words like "Holy Joes" or "body eaters".'

'Where is the altar cross?' I asked.

'That's in the vestry,' he replied. 'Evidently they must have used it as a hammer to break up the two bottles of wine. There's wine all over the place. They haven't touched the safe, so there's nothing stolen. I just don't understand it.'

'The detective in charge is coming to see me tomorrow morning after church,' I said. 'Perhaps he might have some ideas about who is responsible. Certainly it can't be the Reverend Herbert Phillips, who is tucked away safely in Her Majesty's custody. In any case, at least he could spell. At the moment, the only thing we can do is to tidy up the place as best we can for tomorrow's service.'

Between us we put the chairs into place once again and restored the altar frontal to its rightful position, crumpled though it was.

'I think that's enough for the time being,' I told the Curate. 'If you can be here by seven o'clock, I'll bring some candles, wine, and a fresh altar cloth from the parish church. Perhaps you can go down to Dai Elbow and get his assistance before the service. He will be livid, I know that. Meanwhile, Hugh, go back home until then and try and get some sleep, difficult though it may be.'

I put my arm around his shoulders and led him out into the peaceful starry night. 'When you look up and see the wonders of God's creation,' he said quietly, 'to quote the psalmist, "what is man that thou regardest him?"'

Back at the Vicarage, my nostrils were greeted by the scent of bacon frying. 'Another ten minutes,' said my beloved, 'and your supper will be ready. Now then, most important, how are things in Brynfelin?'

'Not too devastating,' I replied, 'but very bewildering. There is no sign of theft or of the consumption of the communion wine. However, there are these weird phrases daubed on the walls, like "Holy Joes" and "body eaters", all misspelt. Obviously not children, but something much more disturbing. It's almost as if there is some strange cult operating on the estate.'

'Well, if it is some strange cult,' rejoined Eleanor, 'their intellectual level is very low if they can't spell such simple words. I shall be more than interested to hear the views of the sleuth in charge when he comes tomorrow. Anyway, come and devour these rashers, accompanied by two fried eggs.'

When I went to bed my stomach would not allow me the privilege of sleep, despite the hard work of the two hens and the sacrifice of the fatted swine. Time and time again I went over the details of what I had seen in St David's, trying to make sense of it. Eventually I succumbed to the charms of Nirvana and temporary annihilation.

The alarm clock brought me to life again to face the demands of St David's Church, the needs for communion wine, candles, altar linen and, later in the day, some white paint to obliterate the crude graffiti on the walls. I shaved and bathed quickly, incurring two or three incisions on my chin in the process. When I appeared at St David's I must have resembled the aftermath of one of Dai Elbow's encounters on the rugby field.

The churchwarden was there, breathing fire and slaughter to the perpetrators of the attack on his beloved church.

'They must be bananas,' he growled. 'What's the point? There are far more "Holy Joes" down in the Pentecostal lot in Abergelly, and as for the "body eaters", our crowd know that it's only biscuits they're eating. They are not cannibals with grass skirts. God help us.'

'The only thing we can do, Dai, is to wait and see what the police have to tell us,' I said. 'In the meantime I expect you will have a bigger congregation than usual. They will all be coming to inspect the damage.'

'I tell you what, Vicar,' he replied, 'I can guarantee they won't find any. I've brought enough white paint to cover any amount of rubbish they've put on the walls, so they'll be disappointed. But it won't be as bad as when that mad parson attacked the church. Now that was really bad. This time we'll 'ave it all under control.'

Throughout the service at St Peter's I found it difficult to concentrate. News of the desecration of St David's had reached the congregation in Abergelly by means of the local radio station. Tom Beynon was incensed. 'We are trying to do the Lord's work up there and what do we get? It's almost as if the devil is determined to put an end to it.'

'It's quite possible that he has disciples up there,' said Ivor Hodges. 'From what I can gather from the press, there are any number of Satanic cults in existence these days, including some in South Wales according to an article I read in the *Observer* last week. I should not be at all surprised if this is the work of some such group.'

'All I can say,' replied Tom, 'is that I should be very surprised. Most of that lot up there don't even know if God exists, let alone the devil.'

'That is fine,' rejoined Ivor, 'but it only requires a handful of perverted people to indulge in such acts.'

'Well, gentlemen,' I said, 'I must leave you to hear what the police have to say on the matter. I shall let you know at Evensong the outcome of the interview. If you remember, the last time the church was invaded they knew a great deal, but somehow I do not think they will be so well informed as then.'

By the time I went back to the Vicarage, the police officer was standing on the doorstep. He seemed to be unusually short to meet the necessary height required for aspirants to the force. 'Ah, Vicar,' he said as I approached him from behind. 'You have taken me by surprise.'

'Do I get marks for that?' I replied.

'Ha! Ha!' he intoned with a dead-pan face. His completely humourless response made me wonder if it was a phrase to be used in the latest police manuals. 'Evidently you have a sense of humour.'

'May I suggest that we retire to my study?'

By now Mrs Cooper had appeared. 'I'm sorry I was late answering the door,' she said, 'but I was in the back part of the house.' I did not enquire what part it was, but her flushed cheeks told the whole story.

'Would you like a cup of coffee?' I asked the representative of the law.

'Yes please, Vicar,' he replied, giving the precise details of his requirement. 'One and a half spoonfuls of coffee and a minimum of milk.'

A bemused housekeeper made her way to the back of the house, trying to remember the needs of the visitor and to decide if I was to join him in the refreshments, since I had not indicated if I would do so. In the meanwhile, I led the officer into the study, where he introduced himself as Inspector Warburton. I ushered him into the armchair opposite my desk and then sat down to hear if he had any information to offer about the crime.

He placed his hat on the table beside him in a deliberate manner, as if he were about to testify in court. 'First of all, may I say, Vicar, that anything I may divulge to you is to be regarded as secret, at least for the time being. Is that clear?'

'Perfectly clear,' I replied.

'Second, may I stress that almost all of what I am about to say is – how shall I put it? – conjectural.' He frowned, as if he were a professor about to disclose his innermost thoughts. 'You may not know this, but there are a number of what are called Satanic cults operating in South Wales. We have knowledge of at least two in this area. At the moment there is nothing tangible to connect them with this incident at Brynfelin, but all our efforts will be channelled in that direction.'

I felt the time had come to ask for definite evidence which would connect the devil and St David. 'I was speaking to my churchwarden this morning,' I said, 'and he told me that an article in the national press last week indicated that there were a number of these cults in South Wales.' His eyebrows arched. 'If there is a likelihood of a connection between these way-out groups and the graffiti on the walls of St David's, how come the artists were so illiterate? Furthermore, why on earth should they choose to attack a wooden tabernacle attended by a few on a council estate? Something doesn't add up here.'

His professional attitude was resumed. The frown deepened. 'That, of course, is the problem,' he said after a pause for thought, which was obviously painful to him. 'What we must do is to find possible witnesses to the incident. My men are engaged in the task at this very moment, doing a house-to-house enquiry. If by any chance someone has seen suspicious activity we shall need a word picture of the suspect. Then we shall be able to compare it with photographs of the known members of the cult. Apart from that there is little else we can do at the moment.'

'You talk about known members of the cult,' I replied. 'What is the social background of the membership?'

Once again there was a pause and a frown. 'I don't think I should divulge this, but since you are a man of the cloth, I would say that they are middle class or lower middle class perhaps, like school teachers, bank clerks, that kind of person.'

'Then how in God's name,' I exploded, 'can you connect the graffiti on the walls of St David's with that kind of person?'

'Ah!' he replied, struck with another avenue of thought. 'They are very devious and could be concealing their identity by deliberately misspelling words.'

'It seems to me, Inspector, that you are as mystified by the break-in at the church as we are,' I said.

'Now, now, Vicar,' he riposted, 'that is uncalled for.' He stood up and straightened his shoulders. 'I shall be in touch with you as soon as we have something positive to report. Good day to you.'

When Eleanor heard the front door slam, she came out from the kitchen. 'Dinner's almost ready,' she announced.

'Well, what news did Sexton Blake bring?'

'He spent about a quarter of an hour pompously disguising the fact that he had no news to bring,' I replied, 'and then departed huffily when I suggested that he was as mystified as I was about the perpetrators.'

'Frederick,' she said, with a glint of merriment in her eye, 'that was very naughty. You never know when you will need the help of the law. I should hate to think that you were in their black books, but I am glad you did it. Come on, love – have a glass of sherry before our meal.'

As we sat in the front room sipping our preprandial tipple, I said to her, 'I don't think this was the work of some dippy middle-class cranks. It's more likely to be the work of some teenager on the estate looking for something to do on a Saturday afternoon. It may be that we shall discover some clues before the experts at the police station.'

The next morning I had a phone call from Ivor Hodges at his school. 'Vicar, I think you had better come down,' he said. 'I have some very interesting news for you.'

'I am about to do a sick communion, Ivor,' I replied. 'I take it that the news is not urgent. If so, I shall be with you in half an hour or so.'

'Oh no!' he said. 'It is not that urgent, but it is important as far as you are concerned.' I found it difficult to keep my mind on administering the sacrament to Miss Sarah Harris, an elderly spinster. After the brief service, when she was accustomed to engage me in conversation at some length, she was dismayed to find that the Vicar was standing at the door and not sitting opposite for a chat.

'Sorry, Miss Harris,' I said, 'but I have an urgent appointment. I'll stay much longer next month. You know how I look forward to our tête-à-têtes.' She had been teaching French in the grammar school in Cardiff until her retirement and loved to indulge in gossip about local politics, not to mention the world in general. On this occasion I was in no mood for a discussion about the shortcomings of the council's educational administration or the standards of teaching in the schools of Abergelly, I wanted to know about the very interesting news awaiting me.

When I went into the headmaster's office I was greeted by Elizabeth Williams, secretary to Ivor Hodges and principal contralto in the Abergelly Gilbert and Sullivan Society. 'Cup of tea?' she enquired. 'The Head is already drinking his.' A few minutes later I was seated in the inner sanctum, drinking tea and anxious to hear what Ivor had to say to me.

'Well, Vicar,' he began, 'I have found the culprit responsible for the desecration of St David's. I am sorry to say that he is a pupil in this school, a 14-year-old by the name of Harry Griffiths.'

'How on earth did you discover this?' I asked.

'He made the mistake of boasting about his exploit in the earshot of his form master, who happened to have entered the room unnoticed by the braggart and his audience. The next minute he had been frog-marched in front of me. His face was ashen, his body was trembling. It was not a pretty sight. He confessed everything. The boy has an unhappy background with a bully of a father and an intimidated mother.'

'Did he explain why he had daubed the graffiti on the walls?' I enquired.

'I thought it best if you pursued that line of interrogation,' he replied. 'I wondered whether I should contact the police at once, but decided that it was best if I let you know first what had happened, then you could decide what to do next. He is in the canteen in the custody of Mrs Whitehouse, the scourge of the lunchtime diners. Elizabeth will take you there.'

On the way there she informed me that Harry was more sinned against than sinning. 'I know the family,' she said. 'Evan Griffiths is someone who is a tyrant, frequently in trouble with the law and the scourge of his three children. Harry is the youngest and so far has not been in any scrape, unlike his two elder brothers. Maybe he felt that it was time that he followed in their footsteps. Probably that was why he was showing off to his classmates when Mr Richards overheard him. Anyway, you can find out for yourself.'

From the overpowering aroma of cooking which resembled that of Rabiotti's fish and chip shop, it was obvious what the pupils of Abergelly Secondary Modern School were to enjoy as their *pièce de résistance*. Sitting on a chair in a corner of the school dining room was the small figure of Harry Griffiths. Anybody more unlikely as a perpetrator of a crime against the established order of society it would be difficult to find. 'This is Harry Griffiths, Vicar,' said Elizabeth Williams, and left us.

The boy studied the floor as if it held a tremendous fascination for him. 'Now then, Harry,' I began, 'your headmaster tells me that you are responsible for the break-in into St David's last Saturday. I have come to ask you why you did this. You have not stolen anything, as far as I know. All you have done is to write some words on the walls of the church which are an attack on the Christians who worship there. That is a serious offence. I suppose you know that the police are investigating the break-in and are calling on all the houses on the estate. I am afraid that you are in deep trouble. It means that you will have to be taken down to the police station for questioning.'

He remained obstinately silent, his eyes fixed on the floor. 'Why did you scrawl the words "body eaters"? Do you think that all the people who come to St David's are cannibals? Look at me, Harry.'

Slowly he raised his head, his eyes averted from my gaze. 'My dad says that when the people who come to church eat the bread they get, they think that they are eating the body of Jesus Christ. He thinks they are crazy.' He spoke so quietly that I found it difficult to hear his words.

'Why should that make you break into St David's?' I asked him. Once again there was a long silence. By now I was beginning to feel sorry for the boy. 'I am only trying to help you, Harry,' I went on. 'The police will be much harder on you than I have been, believe me.'

I was wasting my breath. He spoke not another word.

'Well, I am afraid I have to report to the police that we have found the culprit,' I said, 'and they will be coming to collect you before long.' I left him, sitting huddled up in his chair, a picture of misery.

'Well?' said Ivor Hodges, when I rejoined him in his office. 'What have you decided to do?'

'I am afraid I must contact Inspector Warburton, much as I feel sorry for the boy. I shall have to let the law take its course. I must admit to feeling some unchristian satisfaction that the mighty has been put down from his seat with his theory that what little Harry Griffiths had done was the work of a Satanic cult. Do you mind if I phone him from here?'

'Be my guest, Vicar,' he said.

It took quite a while before I was put through to the Inspector. 'What can I do for you, Vicar?' he asked in somewhat icy tones.

'You can come to Abergelly Secondary Modern School and pick up the culprit responsible for the desecration of St David's Church,' I said, relishing every word. There was a long silence as the officer strove to come to terms with the information. Humble pie is always difficult to digest, especially when the eater is an important officer of the law.

He cleared his throat. 'Er – how did this come about?' he asked. 'My men are still engaged in a house-to-house enquiry on the estate.'

'A 14-year-old pupil in the school was overheard by a master boasting about his exploit to two fellow pupils in the classroom,' I replied. 'Since then he has been questioned by the headmaster and me, and it is a fact that the boy has committed the crime. As the pupils are due to be queuing for their fish and chips in three quarters of an hour, perhaps you could arrange for his transport to the police station in the next half hour or so.'

By now he had recovered his dignity. 'Someone will be at the school in the next few minutes to make the arrest,' he snapped. With that he put the phone down, probably with a slam, at the other end.

'Ivor,' I said, 'I don't think he is well pleased. It is policemen who are supposed to solve crime, not schoolmasters!'

I had scarcely finished my comment on the attitude of Inspector Warburton when Mrs Whitehouse came bursting into the room. ''E've gone,' she announced. 'One minute 'e was there, the next 'e 'ad disappeared.' As all the classes were still in their rooms, it would be easy for him to make his escape. By the time the police would arrive, he could be anywhere. Now I had the unpleasant prospect of eating humble pie, which I found extremely indigestible.

Once again I had to wait what seemed an interminable length of time before I reached the inner sanctum of the Inspector. 'Yes, Vicar?' he said loftily.

It was my turn to hesitate. 'Er – I am afraid I have to report that the boy, Harry Griffiths, has escaped from the school canteen and has disappeared from the school.'

'What!' he exploded. 'When you told me that this youngster was being kept in the canteen, I thought it was hardly a case of safe custody. I shall have to inform all officers to be on the alert. In the meanwhile, there will be two men arriving at the school in the next minute or two. At least they will be in the vicinity immediately.'

When I put the phone down, Ivor said. 'The last thing the boy will do is to make for his home. Knowing the reputation of his father, I am sure he would rather be with the police. Perhaps he will try to hitch a lift from someone.'

'What driver would take a little shrimp like him on board?' I replied. 'He looks more like twelve than fourteen. In any case, what would he live on if he got to a town up north or down south?'

'Since his father and his elder brothers are known thieves,' said Ivor, 'I should think he would be able to cope with what he could steal from a grocery store. He could sleep rough at this time of the year without too much danger to his health.'

'Not for long,' I riposted. 'In any case, the police in all the big towns will be alerted to look out for him. For his own sake, I hope they will find him. I only wish that it had not been reported to the police and that we could have dealt with the situation ourselves.'

'My dear Vicar,' replied Ivor, 'I am sure that this is the best thing that could have happened, both for Harry Griffiths' sake and for St David's. It will do the boy and his family a power of good, especially his father. From now on they will be under the eagle eye of the law. As far as St David's is concerned, they will keep a close watch on the building. I don't think any potential vandals will think it is easy prey from now on.'

A knock on the door from Elizabeth Williams heralded the entry of the two constables who had come to collect the miscreant. 'We have just heard on our car radio that the boy has escaped from the school,' said one of them. 'PC Owen and PC Timothy. Could you please tell us what has happened?'

The headmaster gave an account of the morning's events and of the incarceration of the boy in the canteen. 'If you don't mind me saying so,' commented PC Owen, 'it was asking for trouble leaving him in the canteen. Anyway, I don't suppose anybody has seen him leave the building.'

'I am afraid not,' said Ivor. 'I would have thought that he would have gone out through the back, avoiding the main road, and made for the streets behind the school.'

'At what time would this be?' enquired PC Timothy.

'I should think about ten minutes ago,' replied the headmaster. 'Would you say, Vicar?' I nodded my head.

'In that case, he can't have gone far,' said PC Owen. 'Four wheels are faster than two legs.' With that the pair made a swift exit.

'With a bit of luck,' I said, 'they will find him before he gets into further mischief.'

'Let's hope so,' said Ivor. 'It strikes me that you consider Harry Griffiths more important than St David's.

A few minutes later, as I was driving away from the school, I saw a diminutive figure running pell-mell down Evans Street about a hundred yards from the school. I could not believe my good fortune. I pulled up alongside the fugitive, who was out of breath. 'Hop in, Harry,' I said. 'You can come back to the Vicarage with me. If you don't, the police are around here, waiting to pick you up. Which is it to be?'

Without any hesitation he climbed into the seat alongside me and sat silent throughout the short journey. No sooner had I parked the car outside the door than my wife drew up alongside me, staring at my passenger. 'Come on out,' I instructed him.

As he did so, my wife left her car and came around to meet me. 'And who is our visitor?' she asked.

'This is Harry Griffiths, who will be joining us for lunch,' I told her. 'I shall explain all when we get indoors.' I took the bewildered youngster by the arm and led him up the steps, where a ring on the bell brought our housekeeper to the door. She looked in puzzlement at the trio in front of her. 'Will you please find an extra place for lunch, Mrs Cooper?' I said.

'It's sausages and mash on the agenda for today,' she replied, 'and we've got hundreds of them, so it will be all right.' The prospect of hundreds of sausages for his unexpected meal brought a look of pleasure to Harry's hitherto expressionless face and a look of amusement to Eleanor's visage.

I took him into the front room rather than my study, and my wife followed. 'Now then,' I began, 'this is the young man who broke into St David's, wrote all those words on the wall, smashed the bottles of wine and threw the altar cross to one side. Sit down, Harry.'

Eleanor stared at the boy in disbelief as his little frame was buried in a large armchair.

'He attends Mr Hodges' school and very unwisely boasted about his exploit, only to be overheard by his form master. Also very unwisely, he tried to escape before the police could come to collect him. Fortunately I was driving down Evans Street just as he was running away. So that is why he is here.'

My wife was speechless, but not for long. 'What an exciting morning for you, Harry,' she said. 'Almost as exciting as breaking into a church and doing all those things the Vicar has just talked about. If you will excuse me, I must go and get ready for our meal. Perhaps you can tell me why you did it while we are at the table.'

By now the young criminal began to resemble the male equivalent of Alice in Wonderland. He still had not said one word since I picked him up. His eyes examined the room in minute detail. Then suddenly he spoke. 'Aren't you going to give me up to the cops?'

'I am afraid I shall have to do that later today,' I replied. 'I don't think you realize how serious your action has been. However, if you can tell us at the dinner table why you did this stupid thing, perhaps we can put in a word to avoid you going to prison.'

He lapsed into silence until the time came for Mrs Cooper to announce that the meal was ready. We went into the kitchen where Eleanor was dishing out large portions of mashed potato to accompany the sausages on the dinner plates.

'Tuck into it, Harry,' said my wife as she placed a generous helping in front of the boy. I have never seen a large plateful disappear so quickly. For someone of his size, it was awe-inspiring. After he had finished his meal with a bowl of ice-cream, Eleanor said to him. 'Now then, my lad, tell us how you came to break into St David's and write those words on the wall.'

Whether it was the feminine touch or his full stomach which prompted the confession, I shall never know, but it led to him pouring out his heart.

He had a very unhappy childhood. His father was a bully and a thief who had been in prison on a number of occasions. Harry's two elder brothers had followed in their father's footsteps, and derided him as an innocent who never got into any scrape. They would boast about their escapades. The boys had been taught to look with scorn on churchgoers, whom their father regarded as deluded hypocrites. ''E said 'e couldn't believe that a piece of bread could be somebody's body. They must be daft, 'e said, and that wine could be somebody's blood.'

Last Friday his brothers had taunted him once again about his clean record. " 'You're a bloody wimp,' they said, so I decided to do something bigger than they had ever done. I didn't want to steal but to do something to get into the papers. I think I've done that, 'aven't I?'

'You have indeed,' said my wife, 'but I am afraid that you might have to do something else that they haven't done, and that is to go to prison.'

I looked at my watch. It was half past two. 'I am afraid I shall have to let the police know that you are here, Harry,' I told him. 'I expect they will be here very quickly; but don't worry, I shall do all I can to see that you do not have to go into a remand home.'

'I think I'd rather be there than be back 'ome,' he said.

I went into my study and rang the police station. When eventually I was put through to Inspector Warburton he said, 'I'm sorry, Vicar, but so far we have not been able to find this youngster.' For the second time that day I had the great satisfaction of telling him that Harry Griffiths had been found by me and not the police force. The chagrin at the other end of the line was sufficient to make his reply almost unintelligible.

# 12

Some two months later, Harry Griffiths was in a residential institution for naughty boys, away from the baleful influence of his father and his elder brothers. Janet Thomas was in the last stage of her pregnancy, the subject of gossip among the mean-minded but the object of affection with the caring members of the congregation. The Curate's wife was still presiding at the organ in St David's, but the tight squeeze into her seat would soon become impossible. Fortunately there was a competent deputy available from the ranks of the Gilbert and Sullivan chorus, Myfanwy Howells, a sixth former in Ivor Hodges' school. Since the number of worshippers in the temporary church had increased twofold in the summer, it was vital that the standard of music should be maintained once again. I was fortified in my belief that the inauguration of the Gilbert and Sullivan Society had been a boon to the spiritual life of the parish as well as a contribution to the cultural activity in Abergelly.

It was due to the energetic ministry of Hugh Thomas on the Brynfelin estate that the size of the congregation at St David's had shown such an encouraging leap. He had been assiduous in visiting and in his development of the youth club, the old age pensioners' group and the junior fun club, as he called it. However, he was less than enthusiastic in a commitment he had given to Dai Elbow that he would play at outside half for an invitation fifteen against the Abergelly Rugby Club, in a match to raise money for the new church in Brynfelin. He had not played for a few years, and his time for match fitness was limited by his parochial timetable. The event was just a few weeks away, on the first Wednesday in September.

Moreover, on his mind was the condition of his wife and the effect on her if he was injured in any way. The churchwarden had assured him that he would be treated with kid gloves by the opposition. 'I'm afraid that's one of Dai's fairy stories,' he told me. 'However, it would look bad if I refused to play in a game which was to raise money for my own church.'

'I'm sure that the Abergelly fifteen would not want to injure the beneficiary of the match,' I replied. 'In any case, most of them are your ex-colleagues.'

A much more effective way of raising money was the third plank in Dai Elbow's plan to assist St David's, and that was to approach the heads of industry in the valley for worthwhile donations to the building fund. The Parochial Church Council had suggested that a dinner might be organized, to which the bosses would be invited and where the Vicar could talk of the challenge facing the parish to find the necessary capital to match the half promised by the Earl of Duffryn, within what was now less than nine years. It was decided that this would be held on the eve of the rugby match, the two events combining to give the maximum publicity to our cause. Ed Jenkins, the reporter, had written a few paragraphs in the local press as a warm-up to a much bigger coverage at the time of the September occasions.

All in all, it seemed that the year was going to be an important era for our outreach to the Brynfelin community. '*Ave pro nobis*,' I wrote to my parents in Swansea. I chose that Latin exhortation because it was the title of a devotional song my mother used to sing as a young lady before an operation to her nose put an end to her singing in public.

So it was that I set out on a series of visits to the barons of capitalism and the lesser lords of the nationalized concerns in Abergelly and its environs. I felt that a personal interview would be much more effective than a letter.

My first encounter with the elite was at the head office of the Stevenson Steel Company. Maurice Stevenson had founded the company in 1939 and had made a fortune during the war years which had been multiplied in the immediate post-war period. There were rumours that overseas competition was beginning to have an effect on the firm. However, since the owner had acquired wealth beyond the dreams of avarice, it would be the workers who would suffer rather than the boss. There were other rumours that Mr Stevenson had a penchant for affairs with the young ladies in his employ. Eleanor supplied me with details of his exotic practices which she had heard from her patients. When I told her that I was going to approach him about a large donation to the building fund, she replied that there should be a very big contribution in conscience money. 'The trouble is that a man like that has no conscience,' she said.

I waited in the outer regions of the hub of the activity to be summoned to the presence of the supremo. As I did so, I wondered if the attractive brunette who was typing letters was one of the industrial harem. Then I told myself that I should not indulge in such unworthy speculations. A buzz on the intercom ended my unhealthy thoughts and the next minute I was ushered into the all-important centre of the Stevenson Steel Company.

I had to admit that I was greatly impressed by the tall, handsome, grey-haired gentleman who came to greet me with his hand outstretched. 'Good morning, Vicar,' he proclaimed in deep, sonorous tones. 'Please take a seat,' indicating an expensive armchair opposite his desk, 'I have heard good things about you since your advent, shall we say, to Abergelly. Now then, what can I do for you?'

'As you probably know,' I replied, 'the new housing estate on Brynfelin is part of my parish. It is a concrete wilderness with no amenities within its confines. A year or so ago we erected a temporary building to serve as a church. The council gave permission for its erection on condition that it would be dismantled within ten years, unless replaced by a permanent construction. Since that time, the Earl of Duffryn has promised to pay half the cost of the new church on condition that the parish raises enough money to cover the other half. We have made great efforts to rise to the challenge, including a midnight matinée featuring my brother, which raised a significant sum. However, we are a long way from reaching our goal. It is obvious that we shall need large contributions from within the parish. So we have decided to make an appeal to the leaders of industry in Abergelly. To that end we are arranging a dinner on the first Tuesday in September, at the Celtic Country Club. I have come to invite you to attend. The Mayor will be present and I am hoping that the Bishop will also be there. That, in a rather large nutshell, is the reason for my visit this morning.'

He listened intently to my spiel. After a long pause spent examining his fingers, he asked, 'And what has been the response so far from the other magnates in the valley?'

'You are the first on my list,' I replied.

He smiled wryly. 'I am flattered,' he said. 'One other question. How much is this new church going to cost?'

'I am afraid that so far I have not approached the diocesan architect to draw up plans and give us an estimate of the money involved.'

He raised his eyebrows. 'May I suggest that before your dinner you see your diocesan architect, get plans formulated and a rough estimate of the cost of the building. It is not for me to tell you how to run your business, as it were. I am amazed that the Earl of Duffryn promised to pay half the cost of the building without knowing the sum involved. I suppose that as someone of great wealth, he could regard that as a minor consideration. However, to us leaders of industry, as you called us, any contribution we may make has to be taken from a budget which is finely balanced. Yes, I shall be pleased to come to your dinner. I assume that a formal printed invitation will be on its way in due course?'

'Thank you very much, Mr Stevenson,' I replied. 'I shall make an appointment with Mr Edgar Roberts, our diocesan architect, this afternoon. By the day of the dinner I shall have details of the project available for our guests.

Once again, thank you for sparing your valuable time and for your kind advice, which I appreciate greatly.'

'Don't go overboard, Vicar,' he said.

As soon as I arrived at the Vicarage, I phoned Edgar Roberts. He was about to go to lunch with a client, but the urgency of his appointment faded as he realized that he had a lucrative engagement in the offing.

'I can finish my consultancy by half past two,' he said. 'Will three o'clock suit you?'

'Fine!' I replied.

As I put the phone down Eleanor arrived from her morning duties. 'Well,' she asked, 'how did your date with the steelworks gigolo go?'

'Splendid,' I replied. 'First of all, he will be coming to the dinner but, more importantly, he has put me wise to a number of things. As a result I have phoned our diocesan architect and arranged a meeting with him at three o'clock this afternoon. Apparently our potential industrial donors will require to know what sum of money will be involved in the building of the church. I must say that I felt very embarrassed when Mr Stevenson asked me how much the new St David's would cost and I had to tell him that I had no idea.'

'My dear Frederick,' said my wife, 'Maurice Stevenson must have thought it incredible that you were asking him and his confrères to pay out their hard-won takings on a church which has not been designed or costed.'

'As you know,' I replied, 'I thought it was too early to indulge in details at this stage. Now I realize that the next eight years will soon go.'

'I can never see you as a captain of industry,' she commented.

Edgar Roberts was most effusive when he greeted me at his office in the diocesan centre. 'I wondered when you would be coming to see me,' he said. 'I take it that you will not want anything elaborate – a purpose-built concrete structure like the one at Cwmarfon, for example.' As someone who had sweltered in the heat or been subject to drips from the leaking roof in that building, I replied with an emphatic 'No!' He was taken aback at my vehemence.

'If it means an escalation in cost,' I said, 'it is something that we shall have to face. I don't want a cathedral, I want a brick-built building to hold about two hundred worshippers and I want it multi-purpose, with a kitchen and toilets.'

'In that case, Vicar,' he replied, 'there will be an escalation in cost, as you put it. I am afraid that the grant you will get from the Diocesan Building Fund will be small, in fact infinitesimal in comparison with the cost. I gather that the Earl of Duffryn has agreed to pay half. That still leaves a large amount of money to be raised.'

'I am fully aware of that, Mr Roberts,' I said, 'and I am also aware that we have only a limited amount of time available. However, I feel sure that the parish can rise to the occasion. At the moment all that concerns me is that you give me an estimate of the sum involved within the next fortnight.'

He gasped. 'My dear Vicar, that is impossible. First of all I have to draw up the plans. You will have to get them approved by your Parochial Church Council. Then I shall have to obtain tenders from the various building firms.'

'Before you go any further,' I said, interrupting him when he was in full flow, 'all I want now is a rough estimate of the target facing us. In a few weeks' time I am holding a dinner for the local bigwigs in industry to ask for some large donations to our building fund. It is vitally important that I shall give them an idea of the money we must raise. That's all I ask.'

'All you ask is not easy,' he replied. 'It may be that I shall be considerably out in my estimate when the time comes for the actual building. However, if that is what you want, you can have a very rough sum on your desk in a week or so's time. Remember, it will be very rough.'

'Thank you, Mr Roberts,' I said. 'It means that when I stand up to address the potential donors, at least I shall be able to let them know the size of the financial demands involved in building a permanent church.'

On my way back from my interview, I called in at Tom Beynon's residence to give him an update on what had happened in the past six or seven hours. He opened the door to me, minus his walking stick.

'How nice to see you unaided,' was my greeting.

'And how nice to see you, Vicar,' came the reply. 'I hope to be back at work in a few weeks' time. My missus can't wait for that to happen. Then the house will be her own once again. Women!'

'Come off it, Tom,' I said, 'you would have been in a sad plight without your wife.'

'Believe me,' he replied, 'no one can tell me how much I owe to that little woman. I suppose I said that to show that I was a big man. I am not really. It would be God help me if I had to do without her.'

We went into the front room. He apologized for the fact that we were not in the living room because Winnie was cleaning it. 'Sit down, Vicar,' he ordered, 'while I get you a pint of our valley's best.' On his return, after handing me a tumblerful of Bevan's Best, he said, 'I take it that this is not a social call. Mind, don't get me wrong, I appreciate your coming here, whatever the purpose might be.'

'You're quite right, Tom,' I replied, 'I have to report to you some rapid developments in our St David's building campaign.' I told him of my encounter with Maurice Stevenson and of my subsequent visit to the diocesan architect. 'I am sorry I had to go shopping to Edgar Roberts without your and Ivor's prior knowledge, but I felt that the situation was so urgent that I had to do something immediately. I shall call a meeting of the PCC for next Monday evening.'

'Vicar,' he said, 'as usual you are bang on. We need a leader, not a chairman. I am sure the PCC will approve of what you have done. By the way, I think you had better see Ivor tonight to let him know.'

'I would have gone on my way back, but by the time I had got to the school he would have been on his way home,' I replied. 'In any case, I shall be seeing him tonight at the Gilbert and Sullivan rehearsal. I feel sure that, like you, he will appreciate that I had to act at once.'

I was wrong. When I took him aside at the back of the hall in the break for refreshments, he was not over-enthusiastic.

'I think Mr Stevenson was a little premature in demanding to know what was involved in the cost of building the church. There are still eight years, more or less, before the deadline of the ten years imposed by the council. Any estimate now could be considerably different from what would be the amount necessary then, in view of the fact that building costs are rising rapidly nowadays. Second – I hope you don't mind me saying this – I feel that you have jumped the gun by assuming that you are the sole arbiter in the administration of this parish. Apart from the wardens and the PCC, I would have thought that the Curate-in-charge of St David's should be consulted, since he is the man on the spot. Why is he not here with me?'

'Look, Ivor,' I said testily, 'I shall be having a long talk with Hugh after the service tomorrow morning. Everything has happened at once today, and I had to act on the spur of the moment. I expect that when he knows the circumstances surrounding my decision to get an esti-mate from the diocesan architect, he will see that there was no alternative if Maurice Stevenson was right in what he said.'

It was small wonder that my wife told me at the end of the rehearsal that I was the most uncharismatic Koko she had ever seen. 'You can blame that on my churchwarden,' I told her. When I informed her of my contretemps with Ivor, she replied that she would prefer to place the blame on the steelworks gigolo.

The next morning after Matins, I told the Curate about the interview with the head of the steelworks firm and of the later visit to the diocesan architect. He was surprising-ly enthusiastic.

'Excellent, Vicar,' he announced. 'It may be that we shall have a sudden inflow of money and we can begin to build the church much earlier than expected. What's more, your description of the new building is exactly what I would have suggested. I can't wait to see how soon the dream will become a reality.'

Within the next few days, I had visited eight of the industrial elite. To my great delight they all accepted the invitation to the dinner – some more enthusiastically than others, it is true. Eventually, when I had contacted what Eleanor described as 'those in the second division', we were faced with a bill of £300 or more for feeding the potential benefactors and their wives. As I looked at the menu from the Celtic Country Club, I began to whistle the opening bars of the Lord Chancellor's words in the trio from *Iolanthe*, 'Nothing Venture, Nothing Win'.

'Ever the optimist,' commented my wife as she came into my study. 'The alternative will be the Dead March, if your guests come for a free meal at the expense of the St David's Building Fund.'

'My dear love,' I said, 'if I didn't have any faith, I shouldn't be in this job.'

'There is no answer to that,' she replied.

No sooner had we finished lunch than there was a ring of the doorbell. Mrs Cooper went to answer the call and came into the kitchen to let me know that she had ushered Mr Elbow into my study.

'I am glad you have come, Dai,' I told him. 'I have some good news for you about the big dinner.'

'Well, Vic,' he said, 'I've got good news too, about the rugby match. You'll be glad to know that I've just fixed up the last two places in the side. Bob Smith was on the bench for the Wales A side once. Mind, that was years ago. Anyway, they're all looking forward to the game and they're going to 'ave a run out on the Wednesday before the match. Now then, Vic, wot's your good news?'

'You will be pleased to know that we have all the bigwigs coming to the dinner at the Celtic Country Club. What's more, by then we'll have an estimate of what the new church will cost. I have told the diocesan architect we must have a brick-built, all-purpose church so that it can be used as a community centre as well as a place of worship.'

'Brilliant!' he exclaimed. 'All we've got to do now is to raise the money. You never know, some of those bosses may come up with a fair amount, if it's only to show that what the Earl can do, they can do as well.'

'We'll see, Dai,' I replied. 'My wife tells me that I must not count my chickens before they are hatched. However, God moves in a mysterious way His wonders to perform.'

'I agree with that, Vicar,' he said.

As the days went by, I began to worry about the estimate for the building of the new church. 'Come on, Frederick,' said my wife, 'you are the man of faith, you told me. Now that the moment of truth approaches, it seems that you are getting a bit weak at the knees.'

Somewhat annoyed that my faith was being questioned, I snapped a retort, 'There's nothing wrong with my faith, but there's everything wrong with Mr Edgar Roberts. I should have had the estimates long before now.'

'There's a simple answer to that,' she replied. 'If you were a businessman, you would not have been sitting here biting your nails. You have a phone – why don't you ring him?'

Stung into action, I picked up the receiver and dialled the architect. His secretary intoned, 'Diocesan architect's office, can I help you?'

'This is the Reverend Fred Secombe, Vicar of Abergelly. I should like to speak to Mr Edgar Roberts on a matter of some urgency.'

'Hardly urgent,' murmured Eleanor, as she stood beside me.

I put my hand over the phone. 'Would you mind refraining from interfering with my parochial affairs?' I said heatedly. 'I would never intrude in your medical matters.' She moved away and went into the kitchen singing 'Stay, Frederick, Stay' from the duet in *The Pirates of Penzance*.

The unmusical tones of the architect followed over the phone. 'What is the urgency, Vicar?'

'Mr Roberts,' I said, in high dudgeon, 'in ten days' time I have a most important function to raise money for the building of the new church, in the course of which I shall have to let the donors know the extent of the money involved. The sooner I know, the better, not only for them but for me as well.'

There was a long pause. 'My apologies, Vicar,' came the reply. 'I have had difficulties getting answers from the various builders I have contacted. However, I shall post the estimates I have received immediately. There are still two more to come. I shall ring them and you can have their reply the day after tomorrow. I have indicated in my remarks in the margin of the different documents, as it were, what I judge to be a fair assessment. They will be with you tomorrow.'

I was about to ask him for a rough idea of what we were facing as a financial burden, but what my wife had described as my 'getting a bit weak at the knees' put a clamp on my tongue. 'Thank you, Mr Roberts,' I said meekly and put down the phone. At least, I said to myself, I shall know tomorrow the extent of the challenge the parish will have to face.

I went into the kitchen. 'Well?' enquired my wife.

'In the morning there will be a number of estimates arriving, with two more the day after.'

'And how much roughly will they be?' she asked.

'I have no idea,' I said tersely.

'You aren't half frightened, Vicar,' she replied.

I have never awaited the morning post with so much trepidation. If it arrived as usual, it would be there after I came back to the Vicarage following Matins. Hugh Thomas was due to take the service while I read the lessons. There were a number of Spoonerisms, culminating in the parable of St Luke's Gospel about the man possessed with demons, where I reversed the meaning by reading 'and the first state of that man was worse than the last'. This provoked an unseemly outburst of laughter from my curate. I glared at him. He swallowed hard and began 'Blessed be the Lord God of Israel, for He hath visited and redeemed His people.' The rest of the service continued in a state of high tension as poor Hugh strove to control his feelings.

As soon as we concluded the proceedings with the grace, I was up on my feet while he remained on his knees to indicate his penitence for his inability to control his sense of humour. By the time I was in the vestry divesting myself of my cassock, he had joined me, looking duly contrite for what he called his 'lapse'. I bade him a quick farewell and made a hurried exit to the Vicarage.

When I opened the door there were a number of envelopes on the mat, including a large brown paper packet of what was obviously the enclosure from the diocesan architect. I picked it up, ignoring the rest of the mail, and took it to my study. I was joined by my wife.

'Left the mail for you to savour,' she said.

'Do you know what?' I asked. 'Sometimes I wonder whether you are with me or against me.'

She put her arms around me, lifted up my face and kissed me fervently on the lips. 'There's your answer,' she murmured. 'Does that convince you?'

'So much so that if you were not going to work I would have carried you upstairs,' I replied.

'You naughty man,' she said, 'you can carry on this evening, once the kids have gone to bed and Mrs Cooper is safely tucked away in her little nest. Now then, open that envelope.'

It took me quite a while to open the packet. My hands were trembling as I attempted to unveil its contents. 'If you had let me get to work on this conspiracy to hold you in suspense, I could have revealed its contents five minutes ago,' she said.

'Silence, woman,' I ordered in my best Captain Bligh manner. As I read the first of the estimates, it became obvious that the cost of building the new St David's was going to be a task which would tax the parish to the $n$th degree. The amount staring me in the face was £123,000.

'You have lost all your colour,' remarked Eleanor. I passed her the estimate. She whistled softly. 'My dear love,' she said, 'unless those invited to your dinner have very deep pockets and are prepared to empty them, I am afraid that you will have to abandon your brick building for a concrete replica of the monstrosity at Cwmarfon. That was only £80,000, wasn't it?'

'Over my dead body,' I replied. 'Let's have a look at the other estimates. Perhaps they will not be as catastrophic.'

They were. The smallest was £119,000, while the highest was up in the stratosphere at £147,000.

'Sorry, Frederick,' said my wife, 'I have no intention of standing by and witnessing your dead body.'

'Perhaps the remaining estimates will be smaller,' I replied.

'That is what I call clutching at straws,' she retorted. She was right: the two straws were even higher in cost.

I had the unenviable task of informing the wardens of the financial mountain we would have to climb if St David's Church was to be a worthy home for the congregation.

'Let's wait and see what comes out of the dinner,' was the comment of Tom Beynon.

'You are reaching for the moon,' was the scathing response from Ivor Hodges.

'If we've got to 'ave a concrete church like the one at Cwmarfon, let's 'ave it,' said Dai Elbow.

Poor Hugh Thomas was devastated. When we sat in the vestry after Matins he was almost in tears. 'I had such high hopes that we would have a building which would be respected as the best church in the diocese since the war. To think that we would have to put up with a replica of that tatty thing in Cwmarfon is beyond belief.'

'Well, to quote my mother, let's wait and see, as Asquith said,' I replied.

The days flew by as the all-important dinner approached. The Mayor promised to say a few words, an impossibility which I dreaded. What was more encouraging was a telephone call from the Bishop, who asked if he might address the guests. 'My dear Fred,' he said, 'I feel I must make it plain to those who have positions of power and influence in the valley that this is a project which should have their fullest co-operation.'

I thanked him effusively – and not only effusively, but with a sincerity which came from a deep appreciation of all that he had done for me.

'You are looking happy for a change,' commented my wife as she came into my study. I told her of the conversation I had had with his lordship. 'What a lovely man!' she exclaimed.

'Not only a lovely man,' I said, 'but a very influential one.'

It was a delightful late summer evening as Eleanor and I drove to the Celtic Country Club, which was situated in a wooded valley off the beaten track. A mock-Tudor building, it was the haunt of the social elite of the district. Serenaded by a choir of suitably impressive songbirds, we parked our car alongside some very expensive vehicles which again relegated our latest Ford into the second division. Eleanor had been to Cardiff to buy her evening dress, which could have graced any of the very expensive vehicles. In my clerical evening dress I was proud to escort my wife up the steps of the imposing entrance and into the hall, which buzzed with polite conversation.

We went straight into the dining room to inspect the seating arrangements organized by Sid, the PCC secretary.

The plan of the places was laid out on a large blackboard near the entrance. It was a work of art. At the top table there was the array of the Mayor and Mayoress, the Bishop, the wardens and their wives, the clergy and their wives; Janet Thomas was nearing the end of her pregnancy but was determined to be present for the important occasion. Sid had taken care to group the guests according to their importance.

There was still half an hour before the dinner was due to begin at eight o'clock, so we went back to the hall to greet the throng. The Mayor was making a beeline for the bar, leaving his consort in conversation with Mrs Stevenson. Her husband enquired if I had discovered the cost of the new church. When I told him, he showed no sign of surprise. 'I should have thought the estimates were about par for the course,' he said. 'At least you will be able to make it plain to everybody the extent of the financial burden facing you.'

As he finished speaking to me, the Bishop arrived, breathing heavily after climbing the steps to the entrance. 'Anno domini is beginning to take its toll,' he informed us. 'I must say, Eleanor, that you are looking charming.'

'She certainly does,' added the industrial Don Juan, a compliment not relished by my wife, who made an excuse to leave us. Now we were joined by Hugh Thomas and his heavily pregnant spouse, who looked as if she might give birth at any moment.

'These are exciting times for you, Hugh,' said his lordship. 'A new baby and a new church on the way. Let's hope that all goes well for both.'

Soon we were seated in the luxurious dining room. Dai Elbow was a picture of sartorial elegance in his hired dress suit. 'I'm going down to Cardiff to get the best,' he had told me. 'After all, it is my church that is involved.' Tom Beynon was in his best suit, which had been pressed with loving care by his wife, while Ivor Hodges was in a dress suit from his own wardrobe, one which had done duty on several scholastic occasions.

The dinner was a great culinary success, from the smoked salmon first course down to the orange and grape-fruit mélange via the lamb noisettes with bay and lemon. Add to that the unlimited supply of wine, and it was small wonder that everyone was happy when the time arrived for the commercials.

As the instigator of the proceedings, it fell to me to speak first. I spoke of the challenge presented by the Brynfelin council houses, devoid of any amenities and at some distance from the town centre. I emphasized that the new church would provide a social centre as well as a place of worship. I gave them a description of the pro-posed building, a brick construction, not a makeshift concrete tabernacle. I concluded with the unveiling of the amount of money needed to erect the new St David's.

Next, I called on the Bishop to address the diners. He began by praising the courage of the church people of Abergelly in 'tackling the thorny problem of Brynfelin', as he put it. Looking at the Mayor, who looked the other way, he suggested that 'the civic authority must surely help to assist the church in every way possible'. In a very effec-tive finale, he said, 'If the Earl of Duffryn, from one of the distant shires in southern England, is prepared to pay half the cost of this building, surely those who live and work in the district can rise to the challenge of paying the other half.' It was greeted with enthusiastic applause by those members of the congregation present and a more muted response from the guests who had been the object of the exercise.

The Mayor shambled to his feet to deliver what would have been a long and wandering discourse had it not been for an early attack of alcoholic amnesia, which ended the oratory from the top table.

Suddenly, to my surprise, Maurice Stevenson rose. 'My Lord Bishop, Mr Mayor and Vicar, or should I say Mr Rural Dean. On behalf of all the guests, I feel I must express our appreciation of the splendid dinner afforded us and of the words we have heard from the top table. I think I can assure you that we, the representatives of industry and commerce in the valley, will do all we can to help towards this very necessary fulfilment of a need on the Brynfelin estate.' As he sat down, Dai Elbow's applause continued until the last clap.

The Bishop nudged me. 'Fred,' he said, 'I think we are home.'

As we had our nightcap in the Vicarage, I breathed a sigh of relief as I told my wife of the Bishop's remark. 'I hope he is right,' she replied. 'By the way, poor little Janet was looking very uncomfortable. I should not be surprised if the baby will make its arrival sooner than expected.'

'Hugh was on tenterhooks, too,' I said. 'He is not at all happy about playing in tomorrow's match, especially since he has had the minimum of preparation. I know Dai has been assuring him that he will be treated with kid gloves. I'll believe that when tomorrow comes.'

Tomorrow came, and there was quite a big crowd at the Abergelly ground. I sat in the stand with Ivor Protheroe, the chairman of the club. 'It will be good to see Hugh back in harness once again. That boy could have made the international side, but there you are, our loss was your gain.'

A few minutes later the teams trotted out on the fresh green turf. The announcer informed us that both sides would field according to the programme. My curate was indulging in athletic exercises, ready for the kick-off. As soon as the whistle went the Abergelly outside half dropped out and the ball went to Hugh, who caught it cleanly, only to be tackled by the back row forward, who came flying into him. I winced at the collision; so did my curate. A few minutes later he was being carried off after an examination by the club doctor. 'If you don't mind,' I said to the chairman, 'I must go down to find out what has happened.'

As I went into the dressing room, I heard a voice saying, 'I told you, so much for Dai's kid gloves, I shouldn't have played.' My curate was stretched out in a corner, attended by the doctor, who informed me that he had broken his collar-bone and would have to be taken to Abergelly Hospital to have it set. 'Would you phone Janet, Vicar, please?' Hugh asked. 'She is at her parents', Abergelly 326.'

After I had seen him taken into the ambulance I rang Abergelly 326. His father-in-law answered the phone. There was a note of urgency in his voice. 'Yes?' he enquired.

'This is Fred,' I replied. 'Hugh has been taken to the hospital to have his collar-bone set after a tackle this afternoon.'

'You will be surprised to know that Janet is there to keep him company,' he said. 'She has been taken to the maternity ward. The baby is due at any time.'

Some three hours later, Eleanor and I were at the bedside of a radiant mother with a son in her arms and her husband at her side clad in a hospital dressing gown and with his arm in a sling. 'Well, Hugh,' said my wife, 'I know you wanted to be with Janet at the birth, but you could have chosen a less painful way to get there.'

*Also by Fred Secombe and available from* HarperCollins*Publishers:*

# Chronicles of a Curate

*The first three books in Fred Secombe's entertaining and humorous series, now brought together into an omnibus edition*

Set in the Welsh valleys at the close of the Second World War, *How Green Was My Curate* chronicles the arrival of Fred as a young curate in Pontywen, a village peopled with eccentric and unforgettable characters. From inauspicious beginnings, Fred finds himself settling into the community and falls in love with Eleanor, a strong-minded doctor.

*A Curate for All Seasons* sees Fred as acting vicar, in charge of three churches. He does have help, but that is half the problem. Assistant curate Charles is a walking, twitching disaster area, while lay preacher Ezekiel Evans can sermonize a congregation into unconsciousness. Nevertheless, with the help of Eleanor, Fred still finds time to form a church Gilbert and Sullivan society.

In *Goodbye Curate* Fred is reaching the end of his curacy and Eleanor is about to make an honest clergyman out of him. But, as usual, life in the village is still far from straightforward. A trip to the seaside, a village fete, christenings and weddings provide ample scope for the unexpected to happen, usually with hilarious consequences.

# Chronicles of a Vicar

*A collection of Fred Secombe's three 'vicar' stories, the fourth, fifth and sixth books in his entertaining and humorous series*

Newly appointed as Vicar of Pontywen in South Wales, Fred throws himself into the many responsibilities this post entails. In *Hello, Vicar!* Fred finds himself in trouble with a curate of his own, the Reverend Barnabas Webster, a man in love with status.

*A Comedy of Clerical Errors* finds him trying to cope with his eccentric Welsh village, as he gets entangled in an argument over a sermon condemning corruption in the town council, counsels a young organist, and faces the horror of a fatal accident in the local mine.

*The Crowning Glory* is set in Coronation Year, and it falls to Fred, now a figure of considerable standing in the community, to make various arrangements for the festivities. Fred's happy marriage to the capable doctor, Eleanor, is a source of comfort and hilarity, especially when the rural deanery decides to venture into sex education, with Eleanor placed in the unenviable position of giving the talk.

# The Changing Scenes of Life

Fred and his wife Eleanor have been in their new parish, Abergelly, for eight months and Christmas is fast approaching. The new church of St David's is ready to open but there is a distinct lack of enthusiasm from the local populace. So when Fred arrives at the dedication service to find a packed church and an expectant buzz in the air, he knows something suspicious is going on.

And not for the first time, Fred finds himself in a number of bizarre situations – including a funeral where the departed arrives in a pick-up truck, and a curious incident involving a piano, a hill, and a rather unfortunate sheep.

# Mr Rural Dean

*Mister Rural Dean* finds Fred Secombe three years into his busy life as Vicar of Abergelly. The scene is set with the opening of the Gilbert and Sullivan Society's grand production of *The Pirates of Penzance*. A local venture-and-a-half, it could do wonders for church attendance.

In the midst of first night jitters, Fred finds out that an elderly parishioner has only days to live, a gypsy couple want to be married in his church, and the pirate King elopes with a school-girl member of the chorus.

Then the Rural Dean is fatally injured – could this change everything for Fred?

ρ